Nothing to Lose

Phil M. Williams

Printed in the United States of America.

First Printing, 2021.

Phil W Books.

www.PhilWBooks.com

ISBN: 978-1-943894-78-9

A Note from Phil

Dear Reader,

If you're interested in receiving my novel *Against the Grain* for free and/or reading many of my other titles for free or discounted, go to the following link: http://www.PhilWBooks.com.

You're probably thinking, *What's the catch?* There is no catch.

Sincerely,
Phil M. Williams

For Madison. The world was a better place with you in it. I miss you to pieces. (6-29-1996 – 5-22-2021)

Chapter 1: Twenty-Eight Days Left

Joe Wolfe hit the button on the interior wall, and the garage door opened, letting in the afternoon sun. The garage held his tool bench, tools hanging from pegboards, and a riding mower—its engine cover lifted. He stepped past his mower and down the gravel driveway. In the front yard, cardinals fluttered about the apple trees, chirping and hopping from branch to branch. As he walked, he surveyed his overgrown grass. A feral cat stalked him from a safe distance. It was a calico, with patches of gray, brown, and white.

Traffic was sparse along Big Oak Lane. Joe opened his mailbox and grabbed the stack of mail. He listened to the throaty exhaust of a boxer engine, coming around the bend. The black Porsche 911 Carrera zipped past him, turning left onto Wilshire Lane.

Joe's property bordered Virginia state game lands to the north and east, and Big Oak Lane to the west. To the south was Wilshire Lane, a dead-end street accessing four McMansions, and Joe's nearest neighbors. The lead-footed Porsche enthusiast was Dr. Lucas Sellers, one of the aforementioned neighbors.

Joe returned to his house, a two-story saltbox colonial, with stone facing. He entered the mudroom through the garage. When he opened the door to the mudroom, a beep came from the alarm keypad. He had an ADT alarm system, but it was useless. Joe no longer paid for it to be monitored. He removed his boots before venturing farther. He didn't care about dirt in the house, but it was an old habit that had made Colleen happy.

His phone buzzed with a text. He went into the small kitchen, set the mail on the counter, and removed his phone from the front pocket of his jeans.

DH Lawn Equipment: A new engine for that mower will be $799.99 plus tax. Let me know if you want me to order it for you. I can have it to you next week.

Joe let out a heavy breath and tossed his phone on the counter. He opened the drawer under the counter, revealing the hidden trash can. Then he flipped through his mail, tossing the junk as he went. Grocery store coupons, an offer for homeowner's insurance, an offer to extend the warranty for his truck that had already been repossessed, and a letter from Virginia Estate Liquidations all went into the trash. He kept the bills for his Visa, Mastercard, and Discover Card. He had been paying the minimums on his cards, so he could continue to use them, but that was unsustainable. His shoulders slumped, when he came to the letter from West Clarke County.

Joe opened the letter.

NOTICE OF ASSESSMENT LIEN SALE

STATE OF VIRGINIA
COUNTY OF WEST CLARKE

WHEREAS, on or about January 7, 2017, a Notice of Lien was filed in the Deed of Record of West Clarke County, Virginia, covering the real property herein described, concerning default in the payment of the indebtedness, owing by Joe Wolfe, the present owner of said real property, to West Clarke County.

WHEREAS, the said Joe Wolfe has continued to default in the indebtedness to West Clarke County, and the same is now wholly due, and West Clarke County intends to sell the herein-described property to satisfy the present indebtedness of said owner to West Clarke County.

NOW, THEREFORE, notice is hereby given that on July 25, 2017, between 10:00 a.m. and 4:00 p.m., West Clarke County will sell said real estate located at 6200 Big Oak Lane, West Clarke, VA 22666, to the highest bidder for cash, subject to all superior liens and encumbrances of record. Auction will take place on the steps of the West Clarke County Courthouse.

Joe shoved the letter back into the envelope and placed it in the stack with his credit card bills. He had twenty-eight days to find someplace else to live. He took a deep breath and picked up his phone. He went to his recent outgoing calls and tapped the only name on the list—Emily. The phone rang twice, then went to voice mail. Joe listened to the message he'd heard hundreds of times.

"You've reached Emily Jensen. I'm sorry I missed your call. Please leave your name and number, and I'll call you back."

Joe disconnected the call. He climbed the steps to the second floor. The hardwood under his feet creaked as he walked. He went to the master bedroom. A Berretta 92 handgun sat on the bedside table, along with a framed photo. The photo portrayed Joe and his wife, Colleen, standing on a nearby hiking trail, the Blue Ridge Mountains in the background.

It was ten years ago. Joe's scruffy beard didn't have any gray then. Neither did his wavy brown hair. His body was still wiry, but he no longer recovered from those long hikes like he used to. He would be fifty in a few months, and he was graying from the inside out. His focus wasn't on himself though. Colleen's red hair shimmered in the sun. She held her wide-brimmed hat in her hand. She had been careful to protect her pale skin from the sun. Her mother had skin cancer but had ultimately died of ovarian cancer. In the photo, Colleen beamed, her dimples and straight white teeth exposed.

Joe sat on the edge of the bed, his head hanging. Tears welled in his eyes and slipped down his cheeks. He grabbed the Berretta from his bedside table and placed the barrel to his temple. He closed his eyes and placed his finger on the trigger.

Colleen appeared in his mind. She said, "Do it. It's what you deserve."

Joe set down the handgun and sobbed.

Chapter 2: Good Morning

Pounding on the front door woke Joe from his slumber. Morning sunlight streamed through his bedroom windows. Joe rolled out of bed, wearing boxer briefs and a T-shirt. He grabbed his jeans from the floor, dressed, and walked down the stairs. The front door shook from the pounding.

Joe opened the door to find Lieutenant Harold Flynn of the West Clarke County Police Department. Harold was short and stocky, with thin lips and ice-blue eyes. His bald head resembled a cue ball.

"You've had a week to mow the grass," Harold said, his hand on his holstered Glock, and his lips curled into a sneer. "For the time being, this property is still your responsibility."

Joe stared blank-faced at the code enforcement officer.

"I know what you're thinking. Why bother? You're losing this place in less than thirty days anyway. Right?" Harold raised his eyebrows, waiting for a reply that never came. "I'll tell you why. Fines may not matter anymore, but I can arrest you and put you in jail for up to thirty days."

Joe shut the door in Harold's face.

"I'll be back tomorrow," Harold said through the door. "If it's not mowed, I'm gonna arrest you. This is your own damn fault."

Harold was right. It *was* Joe's fault. The property complaints had started after the second trial. Joe had done nothing to address them, and the daily fines had grown into the stratosphere. Joe had thought they were bullshit. He'd been fined for parking his big rig in his driveway, something he'd done for decades without complaint. His wife's front-yard vegetable garden was another fine. Her chickens. Long grass was a constant battle. He'd receive a fine anytime his hay field of a lawn had grown over six inches in height. Joe had tried to fight the county in court, but he'd lost and couldn't pay the lawyer, who also now had a lien on Joe's house.

Chapter 3: The Grim Reaper

Joe removed the scythe hanging from a pegboard in the garage. He'd only used it a few times. Colleen had purchased the tool, after watching a video of a man claiming that it was a great workout and also an environmentally friendly replacement for the gas-powered mower. It had never replaced Joe's mower though. Not until now. Joe checked the sharpness of the blade with his thumb. He used a whetstone to give the blade a razor-sharp edge. He stored the oblong Crystolon stone in his pocket for ready use.

Joe walked out of the garage, the scythe on his shoulder. He started at the bottom right corner of his property, near his neighbors to the south. His property was six acres, but thankfully most of it was wooded. His lawn was about two acres in size, roughly 87,000 square feet.

He grabbed the bottom grip with his right hand and the top grip with his left. Joe twisted to the right, then to the left, slicing the blade across the grass, cutting a half-moon–shaped swath in front of him. The blade produced a satisfying *schwing* sound.

As he twisted to the right again, he took two small steps forward, so he would cut a new swath of grass when he twisted left. This time the blade didn't cut well, as the angle was off. Joe tried again, getting it right this time, the blade producing the satisfying *schwing*. Each cut was about eighteen inches wide and five feet across. Joe wondered how many cuts it would take to mow 87,000 square feet.

Ten minutes later he was sweating, and the blade no longer cut with the same precision. He stopped and ran the whetstone over the blade a few times, reestablishing the razor-sharp edge.

"Hey! What the hell are you doing? Keep your clippings off my lawn."

Joe turned to his right to see his neighbor, Fred Nielsen, standing thirty feet away on his lush green lawn, complete with perfect diagonal mowing stripes. Joe turned around and checked the trail of clippings behind him. Most of the clippings were on Joe's property, given that he was swiping from right to left, but a few errant clippings had invaded Fred's lawn. Joe put the whetstone back in his pocket and continued to swing the scythe.

Fred marched over to the property line, wearing shorts that only covered half of his pale thighs. His T-shirt did cover his gut, and his white socks were pulled to his knees, like a Catholic schoolgirl. With his block head and stocky build, he reminded Joe of an old Barney Rubble.

Fred frowned and pointed at the ground. "See what you're doing?"

Joe continued to swing the scythe, hoping that Fred might get too close.

"You really are a crazy son of a bitch. Can't wait till you're gone." Fred marched back to his house.

Joe took his swipes, stepping forward eighteen inches at a time. As he moved beyond the property line he shared with Fred, Tera Hensley-Jones appeared, pointing her phone at Joe.

Tera narrated the video. "This is the infamous Joe Wolfe, swinging a sickle like the grim reaper. It's fitting, don't you think?"

Tera's McMansion stood next to Fred's and also adjoined Joe's property to the south. She was middle-aged and average height, with straight gray hair and oval-shaped glasses, but her body resembled a younger woman—or even a younger man. She wore a tank top and short spandex shorts, displaying her muscular thighs, arms, and unusually large hands. According to Colleen, Tera was a CrossFit fanatic.

Joe focused on the task at hand, ignoring Tera and her video.

Tera followed him for several minutes, still videoing. The lack of engagement seemed to bore her though. She said, "Fucking piece of shit." Then, she went back to her house.

Joe stopped and sharpened the blade with the whetstone. He turned around to see his progress. The same feral cat from the day before pounced on a mouse that had been exposed by Joe's mowing. The cat eyed Joe, the mouse dangling from his or her mouth. The cat's belly looked large, like it was well-fed. Joe wondered if it was someone's cat.

***

Hours after sunset Joe now swung the scythe with a head lamp on his head. Each twist of his body sent daggers into his back and abdominals. The pain felt deserved, almost cleansing. His T-shirt, hat, and canvas pants were stained with salt from his sweat. After the last swipe, he tossed aside the scythe and collapsed to the ground. He rolled onto his back, gazing up at the stars, wondering if Colleen was watching.

Chapter 4: Less Than Six Inches

For the second day in a row, Joe was awakened by a pounding on his front door. He rolled out of bed and staggered to his feet, his entire body sore. He slipped on a pair of sweatpants and gingerly descended the stairs. The front door shook from the knocking. Joe opened the door to find Lieutenant Harold Flynn, his fist in midair.

"I see you mowed," Harold said, one hand on his holstered handgun.

Joe stared back, silent.

"You missed a spot."

Joe scowled at the code enforcement officer.

Harold beckoned Joe with his index finger. "Come out here. I'll show you."

Harold led Joe to the back of the house. Joe followed in his bare feet. Harold pointed to the tall grass up against the house. Joe had been unable to mow that close with his scythe, not wanting to damage the blade or the house.

"All grass and weeds must be shorter than six inches in height," Harold said. "You got two choices. I can arrest you, or you can cut this right now."

Joe went to the garage. Harold followed, watching Joe's every move. Joe typed the code on the outdoor panel, and the garage door opened. Joe went into the mudroom and slipped on his muck boots. Then, from the pegboard, he grabbed a corn knife, which was a curved blade about twelve inches long. Joe walked to the back of the house again. He groaned as he kneeled on the ground. He pulled the grass and weeds away from the house and chopped them with the corn knife. Harold stood over him, his arms crossed over his chest, and a smirk on his face.

Ten minutes later, the job was finished. Joe struggled to his feet and glared at the code enforcement officer.

Harold spat on the ground in front of Joe. "You need to clean up all that rotten fruit on the ground in the front yard too. It's not sanitary. I'll be back to check." Harold pivoted and returned to his cruiser.

Chapter 5: The Untended Garden

After the visit from Lieutenant Harold Flynn, Joe went back inside and changed into his canvas pants and put on some socks. His stiff lower back and sore muscles made this an adventure. He returned to the mudroom, laced up his work boots, put on his floppy hat, and stepped into the garage. Joe grabbed a shovel and a metal rake from the wall, then placed them into Colleen's old garden cart. He pulled the cart outside to the front-yard garden. The bright sun warmed his bare arms.

A dilapidated split-rail fence surrounded the garden. Various fruit trees grew along the north side of the garden. The south side was filled with grass and weeds where annual vegetables were once cultivated. Raspberry and blackberry canes, goji berries, and maypop vines grew along the crumbling fence. Overgrown asparagus spears, sorrel, and perennial herbs—such as rosemary, oregano, sage, and thyme—grew on the western edge of the garden. Raspberry canes encroached on the herb garden.

Joe pulled his garden cart to the apricot trees. Fruit flies buzzed about the rotting fruit on the ground. Joe raked the rotten fruit into piles, grunting, a dull pain coming from his abdominal muscles with each swipe. The rake caught on the grass and weeds, making the chore tedious. The same fat cat from the day before stood thirty feet away, watching Joe.

After filling the cart to the brim, Joe pulled it to the woods to his north, his battered body struggling with the weight. He dumped the rotten fruit far enough from the edge that Harold wouldn't likely find it. Joe pulled the empty garden cart back to the orchard. He inspected the ripening peaches and cherries, noting pest and disease damage, but also plenty of good fruit. He filled the cart with enough fruit for a week. Then he went to the herb garden for some veggies, but the sorrel was withering in the summer heat, and the asparagus was large and tough. He found some purslane, oxalis, and lamb's quarters to make a salad out of the edible weeds. Colleen had loved to collect wild edibles. She had allowed many edible weeds to grow in the garden.

Joe went back inside and made himself a tuna sandwich, a "weed" salad, and some fruit for dessert. After eating, he grabbed the half-eaten can of tuna and went to the front porch. The small porch was covered with a roof and large enough for two patio chairs to flank the front door. Joe set the can of tuna on the concrete and sat on a cushioned patio chair about six feet away. He fished his cell phone from his pocket and called Emily. One ring and his call went to voice mail. He listened to her message, then he disconnected the call, and shoved his phone back in his pocket.

Joe surveyed the front garden, picturing it as it once was. Colleen with her big straw hat, digging in the soil, transplanting her prize tomatoes. He pictured her with her bamboo baskets, filling them with more vegetables than they could ever eat. She used to supply the neighbors with produce too, never taking a dime from anyone. The same people who wanted Joe gone now.

The fat cat appeared on the front walkway, twenty feet away, sniffing the air. Joe closed his eyes and leaned back in the patio chair, enjoying the shade. A few minutes later, he opened his eyes. The cat had moved closer, now sitting ten feet away from the tuna. The cat licked its lips.

Joe watched the cat from the corner of his eye.

A few more minutes later, the cat crept closer. It was skinny everywhere but her belly. Joe realized he was wrong about the cat. It wasn't fat. She was pregnant. The cat eyed Joe, as she grabbed a piece of tuna and backpedaled quickly, eating the tuna on the walkway, a safe distance from Joe. She did this several times, until the tuna was gone.

Chapter 6: The Eye of the Beholder

Later that night, Joe took a swig from the bottle of Jack Daniel's. His handgun was holstered to his belt, like a security blanket. If he couldn't take it anymore, the gun provided the option to stop the pain. He opened Colleen's closet and ran his hand over her hanging dresses. He brought a floral sundress to his nose, searching for her scent. It had been over two years. All remnants of her scent were gone. Sometimes when he smelled vanilla, it reminded him of her favorite lotion. He tried smelling a pencil skirt, then some of her cardigan sweaters. But nothing of her was left.

Joe shut Colleen's closet and gulped from the bottle of whiskey. Joe's master bedroom was dominated by the queen-size bed. The floral-patterned comforter was unmade, and the fitted sheet had come off the mattress at one corner. Colleen had been the one who made the bed. Joe had always said, "We're just gonna sleep in it tonight."

Colleen had always replied, "It looks so much nicer with the bed made." Colleen had never forced the chore on Joe though. She had just wanted to make everything beautiful.

His and hers dressers stood on opposite sides of the bedroom. Joe staggered to hers, his mind and body dulled from the whiskey. A painting of their house hung over her dresser. The bottom corner of the painting bore her signature. He ran his fingers over the cherrywood dresser top, making streaks in the dust. Colleen used to joke that Joe was oblivious to dust. She'd arched her eyebrows and asked, "You do know that's human skin, don't you?"

But back then Joe was no slob. He had a place for everything, always choosing efficiency over beauty. He kept the garage, the office, their vehicles, and the kitchen in order, maintaining his tools and machines with perfect precision.

Joe opened her T-shirt drawer and picked up the shirt on top. Multicolored peeps were portrayed across the shirt, with the message, Inside We Are All the Same. Colleen had been a chicken keeper too. Every few years, she'd raise a dozen peeps to maturity, and they'd have fresh eggs to go along with the fresh produce. Joe used to complain that they kept the hens too long after they stopped laying, but Colleen wouldn't let him cull them. Now, he missed the birds. Joe sniffed the T-shirt. It didn't smell like her.

Joe opened her delicates drawer, touching the silky negligees. He pictured her standing before him, a crooked smile on her face, the red negligee low-cut, and barely covering her crotch. He swallowed hard and turned away from her dresser. Joe left their bedroom and shuffled down the hall to her art room.

It was almost exactly as she'd left it, except her easel was missing, along with her nearly finished painting of a monarch butterfly on a milkweed flower. The police had taken it as evidence. Blood had splattered on the canvas and the easel and had pooled on the floor. Joe had cleaned the floor himself, once the police were finished processing the scene. Paintings in various stages of completion leaned against the wall, awaiting Colleen's paintbrush or a frame.

Joe browsed the paintings, stopping and staring at one of himself, sitting on the front porch. He remembered her careful gaze, as she looked from him to the canvas and back again. Her red hair had been tied into a ponytail, and her T-shirt was stained with paint. Joe had complained about all the things he wasn't getting done, while posing for the portrait. Joe had asked, "Why can't you work from a photo?"

Colleen had replied, "Try to enjoy the moment, sweetheart."

Tears welled in Joe's eyes. He wished he could have that moment back. Joe took a swig of whiskey and lurched to another painting. A dandelion with a honeybee. Several paintings were leaning against each other and the wall. Joe moved the dandelion, exposing a notebook-size painting of an eye. It had been drawn in pencil, awaiting paint. Joe picked up the canvas, inspecting the drawing. The large eye had a teardrop at the corner and long eyelashes. Inside the pupil was the silhouette of a couple, one of them holding the other at arm's length, as if their touch was unwanted. Or maybe one had his hands around her neck. Joe imagined his hands around Colleen's neck, squeezing the life out of his wife.

He wondered if that's how she had felt about him.

Joe went down the stairs, leaning heavily on the handrail, tears streaming down his face. He staggered out the front door to the porch. He drained the last of his whiskey and slammed the bottle on the walkway, shattering the glass.

"Fuck you!" he shouted toward his neighbors. "Fuck all of you!"

A light turned on in an upstairs bedroom at the Pratts' home, the first house on Wilshire Lane.

"You wanna watch!" Joe grabbed his handgun from his holster and pressed the barrel to his temple. He clenched his jaw, closed his eyes, and pulled the trigger.

Nothing happened. Joe removed the gun from his temple, immediately realizing his mistake. He looked down at the safety, which was on, as he suspected. *God damn it.* He flicked the lever, releasing the safety. Movement from his left drew his gaze. It was the cat. It sat on the walkway, just off the porch, staring up at him.

"You wanna watch too?" Joe slurred.

The cat still stared, with her big green eyes.

Joe sat on the front step, the gun still in his hand. He hung his head and sobbed.

The cat moved closer, within arm's length.

Joe looked up, locking eyes with the cat.

She meowed quietly. Joe might've missed it, if he hadn't seen her lips move.

Joe set his handgun on the stoop and said, "I miss her."

Chapter 7: Love Thy Neighbor

Joe groaned, his head pounding, as he descended the stairs. Morning sunlight streamed in through the windows. He went to the kitchen and made a bowl of instant oatmeal with peaches for breakfast. After breakfast, he opened a can of tuna, scooped half of the tuna onto a small plate, and placed the can in the fridge. He took the plate of tuna to the front porch, along with a bowl of water. A headless field mouse sat on the Welcome mat. Joe set the food and water on the porch. He grabbed the dead mouse by the tail and flung it into the garden. Then, he sat on one of the two cushioned patio chairs.

The cat bounded through the garden toward the front porch. She stopped a few feet away from the porch.

Joe surveyed the calico cat and her collage of different-colored fur, thinking of a name. "Hey, Patches. Thanks for the present. I hope you're not offended that I didn't eat it."

Patches eyed the tuna and licked her lips.

"You hungry? Come on then."

She stepped onto the porch and ate the tuna. Every few seconds, she peered up at Joe, ready to bolt if he gave her reason.

Joe reached into his pocket and grabbed his cell phone. He called Emily. After two rings, his call went to voice mail. He listened to her message, and, after the tone, he said, "Hey, Emily. It's me. I know you're probably not gonna listen to this. I wish things were different."

Joe hesitated. "I love you, Emily. I wanted you to know that." He disconnected the call and shoved his phone back into the front pocket of his jeans.

Patches swallowed the last bit of tuna. Then, she rolled on her side, showing Joe the white fur on her swollen belly.

"Don't get too dependent," Joe said. "I won't be here too much longer."

Patches looked at Joe, with unblinking eyes.

"If I knew where I was goin', I'd take you with me, but I doubt you wanna be a domesticated cat."

Patches yawned, showing her razor-sharp teeth.

"I'm gonna go to the mailbox. I'll be right back." Joe stood.

Patches jumped up and retreated several feet, her tail low.

"You're fine," Joe said, showing his palms. He walked off the side of the porch, stepping away from Patches.

Joe walked down the gravel driveway to his mailbox. He grabbed several days' worth of mail. He scanned the Pratts' house, wondering if someone saw him last night. Linda Pratt walked her prize poodle to the end of Wilshire Lane, about forty yards away from Joe. Linda was a statuesque blonde in her early forties, who could pass for a former model. She had been Colleen's best friend. Linda saw Joe in the distance and quickly turned away, walking back the way she'd come.

A silver Mercedes convertible drove past Linda, pausing at the stop sign, before turning right onto Big Oak Lane, driving past Joe standing by his mailbox. Tera gave Joe the middle finger, as she drove past.

Chapter 8: Fierce

Joe walked back to the front porch, carrying his mail. Patches sat on one of the patio chairs, enjoying the cushion. She stood, when Joe approached the front porch.

"You're fine," Joe said, sitting in the opposite chair.

Patches sat back down.

Joe patted the stack of mail in his lap. "I don't know why I bother. Nothin' good ever comes." Joe looked at Patches.

The cat stared back.

"Linda Pratt was over there with her dog. Best you stay near the house." Joe paused for a beat. "Tera drove by and flipped me the bird. That woman's a bitch on wheels, lemme tell ya." Joe let out a heavy breath. "I don't know how her husband can stand her. Randall's twenty-five years older than her. Rich retired guy. Used to be in finance. Wanna guess why she married a man old enough to be her father?"

Patches lifted her leg and licked her vagina.

Joe laughed. "I don't think that was why. I'm pretty sure it was for the money."

Patches licked her paw and rubbed her face.

"That's *not* why I think she's a bitch though. It's what she did to Colleen. Tera and Colleen used to work together at the middle school. Well, not together exactly. Colleen was the art teacher, and Tera was her boss and the principal of the school. The problems started when someone yelled, 'Principal Hensley's a bitch.' It was a crowded hallway, so Tera didn't know who said it. Later on, a student told Tera that it was this kid, Justin Franks. Now, Justin was no angel. Lived in a trailer with his mom, who was strugglin'—to put it mildly. He was a handful but an excellent artist. Colleen let the boy stay after school with her to paint and draw, so she had a rapport with him. He didn't like to go home to an empty house."

Patches turned from Joe, her ears twisting toward the chirping birds.

Joe leaned back in his patio chair, gazing at the sunny front-yard garden. "Anyway, Tera was pissed. She pulled Justin out of Colleen's class. Colleen was worried about Justin, so she watched the altercation through her door window. Tera shook Justin, and he tried to push her away, but Tera held on to the boy. Colleen intervened, tellin' Tera to let go of Justin. Tera let the boy go, but she ended up expellin' him for assaultin' her. Colleen fought on Justin's behalf, speakin' out at the hearin' and lobbyin' the school board in support of Justin. Colleen was on her own though. The other teachers were afraid to speak out against Tera. They knew what a vindictive bitch she was. They didn't want the hassle. Justin lost the school board vote, five to four. He ended up in a special school for degenerates. He didn't do so well." Joe shook his head. "Last I heard, Justin's in juvie. Armed robbery."

Patches turned from the birds back to Joe and blinked.

Joe met her gaze. "After Colleen spoke out for Justin, Tera did everything in her power to make Colleen's life miserable." Joe clenched his jaw. "Tera's MO was to collect dirt on people, then to use it to her advantage, when needed. Supposedly, she had dirt on everyone. I imagine she still does. Staff, school board members, custodians, students, *everyone*. Except Colleen. But that didn't stop Tera from makin' up nasty rumors about Colleen and usin' her minions to spread that bullshit around the school and the community."

Patches winked at Joe.

"It wasn't just the rumors either. Colleen always had more duties than the other teachers. She was always short on art supplies. Colleen spent thousands of dollars on supplies every year. She got terrible evaluations from Tera. This went on for years, but Colleen refused to quit or transfer schools. She loved the kids, and she wasn't gonna let Tera push her around. I admired her for her toughness. Most people who knew Colleen thought she was a sweet person, and she was, but she was fierce too. People like Tera underestimated her toughness. Tera tried to fire Colleen by usin' her bad evaluations as proof of Colleen's ineffectiveness as a teacher. I think that's the word she used. *Ineffective.* Colleen eventually made that bitch back off." Joe raised one side of his mouth in contempt. "Gave her a taste of her own medicine."

Gravel crunched under car tires. Patches jumped off the patio chair, hiding underneath. Joe glanced to his right to see a silver sedan creeping up his driveway. Joe assumed the car parked in front of his garage. Joe's garage was on the side of the house, connected to the driveway, but not visible from the front porch.

An attractive blonde wearing heels and a skirt suit walked toward Joe on the front walkway. She smiled as she approached. "Joe Wolfe?"

Joe narrowed his eyes. "Who's askin'?"

She walked up to the front porch, and Patches bolted behind the bushes. She put her hand to her chest. "I'm sorry. I didn't mean to scare your cat."

"She's not my cat."

"Oh …" She craned her neck to get a better view of Patches behind the bushes. "Well, she's adorable."

Joe grunted.

She held out her hand. "I'm Denise Eccles from Virginia Estate Liquidations."

Joe stood with a groan. He stepped off the porch, forcing Denise to step back. He held out his hand and said, "What can I do for you?"

They shook hands.

"Did you receive my letters?" Denise asked. "You have to vacate this property before July 25th."

Joe frowned. "I'm aware."

"We conduct estate sales, so you don't have as much stuff to move, and you can make a lot of money. We handle everything. You just have to let us know what we can and can't sell. You're running out of time, but I think we could still squeeze you in."

"What the point? The county and my lawyers will take everything."

Denise furrowed her brow. "I'm sorry to pry, but why not file for bankruptcy?"

"County fines can't be discharged in bankruptcy."

Denise reached into her purse and handed Joe her business card. "If you change your mind, let me know."

Chapter 9: I'm Not a Good Person

Late in the afternoon, Joe set a half-eaten can of tuna and a bowl of water on the porch. He sat in one of the patio chairs. Patches bounded to the front porch from the garden. She meowed and ate her food, only a few feet away from Joe.

"You would've loved Colleen," Joe said. "You'd have cat food and a special bowl just for you. Probably would've bought you a little house with a heater for the winter. Hell, she would've let you inside."

Patches ate her tuna, as if she hadn't eaten in weeks.

"Colleen was that way. Always wantin' to help. I would've told her to stop feedin' you because you'll become too dependent." Joe chuckled. "And here I am doin' exactly that."

Patches looked up from the empty tuna can and licked her lips. Then she sauntered to Joe and rubbed against his leg.

Joe bent over in his chair and petted the cat lightly on her head and back. Her fur was soft to the touch. "You're startin' to trust me. I'm not sure you should."

Patches purred, as Joe stroked her neck and back.

"I'm not a good person, Patches. You wouldn't like me, if you knew what I did."

The cat eyed Joe.

"You really wanna know?"

Patches blinked.

"All right." Joe took a deep breath. "We had this real bad fight."

Patches walked a few feet away from Joe and flopped on the porch, showing her swollen belly.

Joe leaned back in his chair. "I was depressed. I don't know why. I go through waves of depression. I've always been like this. Colleen knew what I was like when she married me, but now she wanted me to see a therapist. I refused. She threatened to divorce me if I didn't. I was pissed. I felt like she was blackmailin' me, and I told her so. I wasn't nice about it either. She said I was turnin' into my father. I think that's what sent me over the edge." Joe swallowed hard. "I grabbed her and pushed her to the ground. She hit her head on the edge of the coffee table." Joe closed his eyes, envisioning the scene. Colleen on the floor, unmoving. Blood pooling on the carpet. Joe opened his eyes, and a tear slipped down his cheek. "I remember the blood and seein' her layin' on the carpet, but I don't remember pushin' her. It was like I was temporarily insane. I wrapped her head in a towel and called for an ambulance. She was still breathin', but I was so afraid that I had killed her. The cops showed up before the ambulance, which surprised me. Linda Pratt had called the police. She had seen us arguin' through the window."

Patches stood and walked to Joe, rubbing against his leg again.

Joe wiped his eyes with his index finger. "Colleen had a serious concussion, but she recovered, thank God. I pled guilty to simple assault, and I went to prison for six months. I thought we were finished, but Colleen was so forgivin'." Joe leaned over in his seat and petted the cat again.

Patches purred in response.

"We reconnected near the end of my prison sentence. I agreed to see a therapist. She agreed to give our marriage another chance. When I got out of prison, I only had a week with her ..."

Chapter 10: Pratt Party

On Saturday night, Joe sat in a patio chair, and Patches lay on the opposite chair. Her ears tilted toward the music coming from the neighbors' house. A citronella candle kept the mosquitoes at bay.

"That's the Pratts," Joe said, gesturing toward their house and the lights in the distance. "They have a party almost every Saturday night."

Patches searched the darkness for prey but was too satisfied or too comfortable to give chase.

"Elliot Pratt's a big-time real estate developer. He's in love with his house. It's the most extravagant house I've ever been in. Must be at least ten thousand square feet. It's like a palace. They have their parties in the basement. They have a wet bar down there. Pool table. Big-screen TVs. Built-in sound system. It's ridiculous."

Patches yawned.

"I know. Big deal, right? I never liked goin' over there, but Colleen was best friends with Linda Pratt. I think I told you that already. Anyway, I hated goin' over there. I'm introverted, like you, but Colleen was an extrovert. She loved the Pratt parties. We used to argue about goin' over there."

Patches stared at Joe.

"You must be thinkin' I have a stick up my ass, but I was right about the parties. The last one I went to, somethin' happened that really pissed me off." Joe swallowed hard. "It was late, and I was ready to leave, but Colleen was talkin' to Lucas Sellers. *Dr.* Lucas Sellers. The pompous ass always wanted everyone to call him doctor. I purposely called him Luke. Anyway, I went to the bathroom. On my way back to the bar area, as I came around the corner, I saw Lucas talkin' to Colleen. From the tilt of his head, it looked like he was starin' at Colleen's chest, but I wasn't sure. I'd had a few drinks. Colleen had worn a low-cut shirt that night, and the look on her face was shock. She saw me first. Lucas's back was to me. He noticed her noticin' me. Lucas turned around, smiled, and said somethin' like, 'Hey, Joe. We were just talkin' about gardenin'. Your wife thinks she can turn my black thumb green.' I looked at Colleen, and she smiled and said somethin' like, 'Anyone can garden. All it takes is love.'

"We left shortly after that. On our way home, I asked Colleen what Lucas had said to her. She had said, 'It didn't matter.' It was obvious that she didn't wanna tell me, so I pushed and pushed. She eventually told me. You wanna know what he said to her?"

Patches blinked at Joe.

Joe shook his head. "It's bad. For the record, I don't like this kinda talk. It's disrespectful." Joe pursed his lips. "He said, 'I'd like to put my dick between your tits.'"

Patches turned away.

"I know. And I never did anything about it. Colleen deserved better."

Chapter 11: Go

On Sunday morning, Joe stepped onto his front porch, carrying a plate of chopped up bologna and a bowl of water. He scanned the garden for Patches. Beyond the garden, he spotted the cat bounding toward the neighbors to his south.

Joe set down the water and bologna. He walked through the weedy garden to the field that he'd just cut with Colleen's scythe. Scattered clouds were overhead, threatening rain. He followed Patches to the dark green grass that delineated Joe's property from Fred Nielsen's. Patches dug in Fred's flower bed. She pooped in the hole and covered it with fresh mulch. Joe laughed and walked back to his house.

Several minutes later, Patches joined Joe on the front porch. As she ate her bologna, Joe sat in his chair, talking her ear off.

"I'd be careful about Fred's yard down there. He's seriously anal about his lawn. I wouldn't put it past him to poison you."

Patches continued to eat, unconcerned about Fred.

"Fred's a county supervisor. Works hand in hand with Elliot Pratt. There's a reason Pratt Property Development's gotten so big. Apparently, Fred makes sure Elliot's zonin' and buildin' permits are all approved. I'm sure Fred gets a nice kickback. Nobody builds around here without Fred's approval. If your name's not Elliot Pratt, Fred makes it real difficult. Guy's a total asshole." Joe hung his arm off the side of the chair.

Patches finished the last of her bologna and walked over, rubbing her head against his hand.

Joe petted her. "Fred and Elliot are friends with Lieutenant Flynn, the code enforcement officer. I think they're the reason the county has been on my ass for every little thing I do. It all started after the second trial. Everyone wanted me gone." Joe blew out a breath. "I never thought they could run up fines like they did. I thought I could fight the county, but I was wrong. There's no fightin' the government. There's only losin'. The only thing I learned is how powerless I am." Joe smirked at Patches. "Now that I think about it, I'd like to take a shit in his flower beds too."

Patches meowed and flopped on her side, now out of reach of Joe's hand.

Joe thought about Elliot Pratt, Fred Nielsen, Lucas Sellers, and Tera Hensley-Jones. "Maybe I should shit in all their flower beds. What do you think?"

Patches yawned.

"What do I have to lose? A little vandalism might be fun."

Patches stared at Joe.

"I know it won't stop the foreclosure. I can't fix that. It's too late."

Patches still stared, her green eyes still.

"Don't judge me. They ruined my life." Joe paused for a beat. "You think I ruined my own life, don't you?" Joe glared at Patches. "You think I killed Colleen, don't you?"

Patches turned away from Joe.

"Don't turn your back on me. For your information, I wasn't convicted. I wasn't acquitted either, but ..." Joe shook his head. "Look. I'm gonna be straight with you. It was two hung juries, and the state didn't go for a third trial, but the whole county thinks I'm guilty." Joe hung his head, tears welling in his eyes. "I don't remember killin' her, but sometimes I have this vision of my hands around her neck. I worry that it's like the last time, when she hit her head."

Patches bolted from the porch.

Joe raised his gaze and called out to Patches. "Go ahead and leave! Everyone else does." Joe ran his hand over his face. "God damn it." He thought about the latex gloves that the police found in his garage trash can. *If I didn't do it, how did Colleen's blood end up on my gloves?*

Chapter 12: She's Back

Four days later, Joe sat on his front porch, scanning the garden and field for Patches. A flash of gray came from the field. Patches slipped through the dilapidated split-rail fence to the garden. Then she bounded to the porch, and rubbed against Joe's leg. She appeared thinner.

Joe bent over in the chair and petted the cat. "Hey, Patches. I wasn't sure if I'd see you again."

Patches rubbed her head against his hand.

"Looks like you had your babies? You must be starvin'." Joe stood from the chair. "I'll be right back."

Joe went inside and prepared a full can of tuna, placing the tuna on a plate, and cutting it into bite-sized pieces with a fork. He returned to the porch with the tuna and a bowl of water.

Patches meowed and stood on her hind legs when she smelled the tuna.

Joe set the food and water on the porch. "There you go."

Patches took big bites.

Joe sat in the chair again and turned to the cat. "Look. I'm sorry for yellin' at you. I got some problems to work out. That's not your fault. I won't do that again. I promise."

Patches continued to eat.

"Thanks for not holdin' a grudge." Joe hesitated for a moment. "For the record, I didn't do it. I need you to believe me."

Patches purred as she ate.

Joe turned from Patches to Colleen's sunny garden. He took a deep breath. "It happened a week after I got out of prison. We were doin' good. We'd already been to the therapist, and we'd had a good session. Bein' away from Colleen and this house made me realize what I had." Joe swallowed hard. "I ran some errands. The hardware store. The gas station. I even went to the grocery store for Colleen. When I came back, I expected her to greet me, but I didn't hear anything. I thought maybe she took a nap, so I didn't call for her. I put away the groceries, then I went to our bedroom, lookin' for her. The bed was made. Then I checked her art room." Joe slumped his shoulders and hung his head. "She was on the floor, a pool of blood comin' from the back of her head. It felt exactly like the last time—when I pushed her, and she hit her head—except this time she wasn't breathin'." Joe turned to Patches again.

The cat lapped at her water with her pink tongue.

"Before I left, she was starin' out the window. She looked sad. I asked her what was wrong. She said, 'When you get back, I need to talk to you about somethin' important.' I asked her if I did somethin' wrong. She said, 'No.' Then she said, 'I love you.' She hadn't said that in a long time."

Patches sat on her hind legs and eyed Joe.

"Part of me wanted to talk right then, but hearin' her say I love you? I didn't wanna ruin that feelin'. In my bones, I felt that what Colleen was fixin' to tell me was gonna change everything."

Chapter 13: The Secret Spot

A woodpecker tapped on a nearby tree. A squirrel scurried up a maple tree. Joe hiked on a game trail through the Virginia state game lands. He followed a familiar trail that he and Colleen used to hike. He had accessed the trail from his backyard, where his property bordered the game lands.

Joe hiked for an hour. Beams of sunlight pierced the hardwood tree canopy. The forest was a mixture of maple, birch, ash, and basswood. Serviceberry and mountain laurel grew in the understory. A red-tailed hawk screeched overhead. At a familiar creek, Joe veered off the trail, following the shallow creek for one-quarter mile. Raspberries and blackberries grew along the stream. Joe picked a few berries, eating them as he went. He eventually turned from the creek and walked uphill to an abandoned hunting cabin.

The stone cabin was small, the size of a shed. It had a door, two broken windows, and a separate outhouse. Trees crowded the little cabin. Joe ran his hand over the stone wall. He entered the cabin, the wooden door unlocked. The floor was dirt. Two old coolers were buried in the floor, as makeshift root cellars, only their lids visible. A fireplace was on one end. A metal bed frame sat at the other end. Light filtered through a few small holes in the roof.

Joe opened one of the coolers, half expecting to find a snake den. It was empty. He surveyed the room, remembering the first time he'd been there with Colleen. *How long ago was it? Fifteen years? Longer?* They'd been hiking in the early spring. With no leaves on the trees, Colleen had spotted the cabin from a distance. It had been in better shape then, but it had appeared abandoned. They'd made love in the cabin that day. "Going to the cabin" eventually became code for "making love." They'd fixed up the place and used the cabin for many years, like a secret getaway, until one day their things were gone. Their food, furniture, fireplace apparatus, blankets—everything except for their old coolers. They never went back after that, their secret spot spoiled.

Joe thought, *You never know when things are gonna end.*

Chapter 14: Nothin' to Lose

"How's motherhood goin'?" Joe asked, sitting in a chair on the front porch.

Patches lay on her side, purring and licking her lips from her meal.

"Don't hang out with me if you got babies to attend to. You won't hurt my feelin's if you gotta go."

Patches blinked.

"Well, I'm sure you know what you're doin'."

Joe turned from Patches and surveyed the garden and field. Fred Nielsen marched through the field toward them.

"Here comes trouble," Joe said.

Fred searched for a break in the spilt-rail fence. He stepped over the dilapidated fence and walked through the garden toward the front porch.

Patches stood and crouched, ready to bolt.

"Don't worry. I'll handle this." Joe stood and stepped off the porch, meeting the old man on the front walkway. "What the fuck do you want?"

Fred glared at Joe, his lower jaw jutting forward. He pointed at Patches on the porch. "That cat's been shitting in my mulch and pissing on my flowers."

Joe glanced back to Patches. She bolted behind the bushes. "Look at it from her point of view. You have the nicest flowers and the freshest mulch."

"That's a code violation. You need to control your animal."

Joe frowned. "She's a feral cat, Fred. You see a collar on her?"

Fred narrowed his eyes at the water bowl and the empty plate on the porch. "If you're feeding her, that's a code violation too. You're going to do something about that cat."

Joe spat on the ground, perilously close to Fred. "Get the fuck off my property."

Fred clenched his fists.

"Make a move, old man. I got nothin' to lose."

Fred's face turned beet red. "This won't be your property for long." He turned and walked away, leaving the way he came.

Chapter 15: Patches

The next morning, Joe sat on the porch, waiting for Patches. After a long wait, Joe stood from his chair and called for the cat. He stepped off the porch and walked into the garden, calling for the cat. He ventured beyond the garden to the field, still calling out for the cat, but he saw no sign of her.

Joe surveyed Fred Nielsen's house, worried that he'd done something to Patches. *He wouldn't kill a cat for pissin' on his flowers. Would he? Maybe somethin' happened with the kittens?* Joe went back to his house, thinking that Patches wouldn't miss dinner.

***

The setting sun was low on the horizon, casting an orange glow over the land. Joe stood on the porch, holding an open can of tuna. "Patches! It's dinnertime. Patches!" Joe set the tuna on the porch and walked out to the garden. He checked the garden, then the field, but still no sign of the cat.

Joe stood on the edge of his property, a single step from Fred Nielsen's dark green lawn. Joe scanned Fred's lawn and landscape. The holly hedges were clipped into perfect boxes, and the juniper trees were shaped into perfect spirals. The lawn was freshly mowed, the mower leaving diagonal stripes. Joe walked through Fred's yard to the front of the brick-faced McMansion. No sign of Patches in the front yard either.

The trash can was on the curb. Joe looked left and right, checking the neighbors. They all had trash cans at the curb too. Nobody was outside on that Sunday evening.

Trash day is tomorrow. Joe walked to Fred's trash can and opened the lid. Three bags were inside. Joe reached into the trash can and removed all three at the same time. Two bulged with trash. One was heavy but had little in it. Joe opened the mostly empty trash bag to find a tied-up grocery bag inside. Joe's heart pounded as he spotted gray fur at the top of the cat-size bag. He untied the bag to find Patches, her body stiff. Dried blood matted her fur on her side, the blood coming from a .22 caliber bullet hole. Another .22 caliber bullet hole was on the back of her skull.

Joe sat on the curb, cradling the cat. Tears welled in Joe's eyes and overflowed down his cheeks. Minutes later, the tears were gone, leaving a residue of rage. He clenched his jaw and stood from the curb. He stalked to Fred's front door, trekking through his lawn, spoiling the perfect stripes.

Joe banged on the door with his right hand, still holding Patches with his left.

Chick-chuck.

The door opened, and Fred appeared, pointing a shotgun at Joe's head.

Joe stood firm, not reacting to the shotgun.

Fred said, "Now it's your turn to get the hell off *my* property."

Fred's wife, Joan, stood a few feet behind Fred, gaping at the scene. She was short and chubby, wearing high-waisted jeans and an oversize T-shirt.

"You're a fuckin' piece of shit, Fred," Joe said, his face twisted in disgust.

"It's your turn to make a move," Fred replied, the shotgun still levied at Joe. "Go ahead. Give me a reason."

Joe inched closer to the barrel of his shotgun. "You think I give a shit whether I live or die?"

"Shut the door, Fred," Joan shrieked. "He's crazy."

Joe looked over Fred's shoulder at Joan and held up Patches. "Your husband killed a defenseless animal. I'm not the crazy one. She has ..." Then Joe thought about the kittens.

Sweat beaded at Fred's hairline. "If you don't get off my property, I'll put a hole in your head."

Joe pivoted and ran home, cradling Patches like a football, and thinking about where she might've stashed her kittens.

Chapter 16: BK

Joe sprinted home and put Patches in the freezer, with the intention of burying her later. Then, he grabbed a flashlight and went back outside. He searched close to his house first, carefully checking the bushes with his flashlight. No kittens in the bushes. Joe moved out from the house, searching in concentric rings, reasoning that Patches would've stashed the kittens close to the house.

For several hours, he frantically looked for the kittens and listened for their meows. He scoured his entire property. He even checked the edge of the game lands, although he doubted Patches would've stashed the kittens there. His flashlight dimmed. Joe hurried back to the house to get a new battery. On the way, he heard a squeaky meow. Joe followed the meow to the overgrown asparagus patch. He shone his flashlight into the dense patch of tall asparagus spears. They branched at the top, like little trees.

Joe saw a little lump of gray and another lump of white and brown. He reached into the asparagus patch and extracted the brown-and-white kitten. It wasn't moving or breathing. Joe then extracted the gray kitten. It meowed when Joe picked it up. It easily fit in the palm of his hand. Its body was gray, with tabby stripes, but the fur on its face and feet were white. Its eyes were closed.

He took both kittens inside, placing the dead kitten with Patches in the freezer. Joe found a box and a blanket for the live one and set the kitten inside. He did a Google search on how to care for a newborn kitten on his phone. Then, he rushed from the house, taking Colleen's bike to the grocery store a few miles down the road.

Soaked with sweat, he parked the bike against the building and hustled inside. He jogged to the pet section. Customers and workers gaped at him. He found a small bottle and powdered kitten-milk replacer. Joe paid with a credit card, pleased it wasn't declined.

Then, he got on his bike and pedaled as fast as he could back home. He rode into his open garage and ran inside to the kitchen, where the box with the kitten sat on the table. The kitten meowed over and over again.

"I'm gettin' there." He mixed the powdered milk with warm water in the bottle. He squirted a little on the back of his hand to make sure it wasn't too hot. It reminded him of Emily as an infant. Joe sat at the kitchen table. He cradled the little gray kitten in one hand; the other held the bottle to its mouth. It meowed, when Joe touched its face with the nipple of the bottle. Then, it opened its mouth and suckled. Joe breathed a sigh of relief and said, "There you go, Baby Kitty."

Chapter 17: A Piece of Her

The next morning, Joe set Baby Kitty back in her box with her blanket. Joe was pretty sure it was a her. He had also searched how to tell the sex of a newborn kitten. He had lifted her tail and judged the shape of the opening below her anus.

Baby Kitty was already asleep, content, and well-fed. Joe rubbed his red eyes. He'd slept in fits and starts, waking every two hours by alarm to feed the kitten and to help her urinate and defecate. Overnight, as he'd fed Baby Kitty, he thought about Emily. He'd wondered if he could ever make it right with his daughter. He'd come to the conclusion that he didn't know and that he needed more time. The foreclosure was coming. He'd soon be homeless and destitute, unless he made some money.

Joe stood from the kitchen table and stepped to the counter. He opened a drawer and riffled through the old mail he'd stashed inside. He found the business card for Denise Eccles from Virginia Estate Liquidations.

Joe tapped the number on his cell phone.

"Hello, this is Denise Eccles."

Joe leaned on the kitchen counter. "Hi, Denise. This is Joe Wolfe. Not sure if you remember me."

"Of course I do." Her tone was upbeat. "How can I help you?"

"I'd like to do an estate sale, if it's not too late."

"That's great. I'll have to check the schedule for dates, but I'm sure we can squeeze you in."

"What happens now? What do I need to do?"

"I need you to sign some paperwork, but that's just a few signatures. The most important and time-consuming thing I need you to do is to separate the things you wish to sell from the things you don't. Normally, we send a team over to help move things for you, but we won't have any movers available for a few weeks."

"That's okay. I'd rather do it myself."

"Great. Just put all the things you don't want to sell in a few rooms that we can keep shut."

***

Joe opened Colleen's closet. He ran his hands over the hanging clothes, thinking about whether or not he wanted to save anything for sentimental value. Then he thought of Emily. He reached into his pocket, grabbed his cell phone, and called his daughter. It went to voice mail after two rings.

After the message, Joe said, "Hey, Em. I'm havin' an estate sale, and I just wanted to know if you want anything. Furniture. Your mom's clothes. Anything you want. Please call me back. I love you." Joe disconnected the call and hung his head. *Who am I kiddin'? She's not gonna call me back.*

Joe went back to the closet, wishing Colleen's clothes still smelled like her. He thought about what Colleen was wearing right before she died. Not what she was wearing *when* she died. Those clothes were still with the police as evidence. *What was she wearing the day before? Maybe they still smell like her. We went for a hike. It was October. The weather was cool but not cold.* He pictured her wearing a light jacket. *A windbreaker maybe.* Colleen had several light jackets. One was a black North Face jacket that was waterproof. She also had two fleece jackets—one light-blue and the other purple.

Joe scanned the closet, finding her jackets. He leaned into the North Face jacket, inhaling, hoping to smell her, hoping to remember her. It didn't smell like anything. He tried the purple fleece jacket. Nothing. He grabbed the blue fleece jacket, bringing the jacket toward his nose. As he did so, he felt something rigid in his hand, where he had gripped the jacket at the breast. Joe checked the inside zipper pocket. A folded envelope was inside. He removed the envelope and unfolded it. No name was on the outside. The seal had been broken. Joe opened the envelope and retracted a single sheet of unlined paper. It was a letter written in beautiful cursive.

Colleen,

I'm so very sorry for what I did after the party. I was wrong to try to touch you. You were very clear about wanting to fix your marriage. I didn't respect your boundaries. For that I am very sorry.

It's just that I love you more than life itself. I don't think I can live without you. When we were together, it was like I was seeing color for the first time in my life. Now everything's black-and-white again. I miss you so much. How do I go on without you?

Please tell me that you loved me too. Please tell me that it wasn't all in my imagination. If I can't have you, please give me something to hold on to.

I love you with all my heart. I'll be waiting. Always.

Joe flipped over the letter, checking for a signature, but it was blank.

Chapter 18: Connecting Dots

Joe took the letter downstairs to the kitchen. He peered into the cardboard box on the table to check on Baby Kitty. She was still sleeping. Joe set the note on the table next to Baby Kitty and her box.

"I think I found out what Colleen wanted to tell me." Joe clenched his fists. His entire body was taut. "She was havin' an affair. You spend your life with someone, and you think you know 'em, but you don't. You never really know anyone." Joe paced in the kitchen. "I was a fool, BK. A total idiot. I didn't see it. Maybe I didn't wanna see it." Joe continued to pace, the wheels turning in his mind. "If I missed this, what else did I miss?"

Joe sat at the kitchen table and snatched the note from the tabletop, rereading the cursive. "The guy talks about touchin' her after the party. That has to be the Pratts' party. Colleen wasn't goin' to other parties, as far as I know. If it was the Pratts' party, it would have to be Elliot Pratt, Lucas Sellers, or Fred Nielsen. Sometimes they have other friends there, but those three are regulars. What do you think, BK?" Joe looked into the box.

Baby Kitty was still asleep.

"You're right. I can't picture Colleen with Fred. They're polar opposites, and he's way too old for her, not to mention what he did to your mother. Colleen would never be with someone who abused animals." Joe reached into the box and petted the cat with his index finger. "Don't worry, BK. We'll make him pay for what he did." Joe retracted his hand from the box and blew out a breath. "That leaves Elliot or Lucas. Lucas sexually harassed Colleen, so my money's on Elliot." Joe closed his eyes, envisioning Elliot and Colleen having sex. He opened his eyes and slammed the side of his fist on the letter.

Baby Kitty meowed.

"If Elliot wrote this letter, he sounds obsessed with Colleen. You think he might've been obsessed enough to kill her?"

Baby Kitty meowed again.

"So do I."

***

Later that afternoon, Joe dug a small grave in the garden. Dark clouds converged from the east and west. Baby Kitty lay in her box nearby, cuddling with her blanket. The soil was loose and black. Beneath the humus layer, Joe dug into the heavy Virginia clay.

Once he'd dug several feet deep, he placed Patches and the brown-and-white kitten into the hole. He picked up Baby Kitty, holding her in both hands, like an offering.

"Is there anything you wanna say?"

A gust of wind blew through the garden.

Baby Kitty shivered and meowed.

"Okay. I'll do it." Joe covered BK in his hands and brought her close to his body for warmth. "Patches was a great friend. She accepted me, when nobody else would." Joe swallowed hard and bowed his head, as if in prayer. "She saved my life. If it hadn't been for her, I wouldn't be here. She was selfless, a great listener, a great mother, and a great cat. The world was better with her in it."

Thunder crackled in the distance.

Chapter 19: Searching for the Author

The next morning, Joe sat on a lawn chair at the end of his driveway, watching the cars go by. The morning sun was low on the horizon. It was in the sixties that morning. Joe wore a sweatshirt with a front pocket. Baby Kitty slept inside. He kept his eye on Wilshire Lane to his south. A black BMW sedan stopped at the end of Wilshire. Then, it turned right, driving past Joe on Big Oak Lane. It was Dr. Lucas Sellers. He also drove a black Porsche, but that wasn't his daily driver. A few minutes later, Elliot Pratt drove his Lexus past Joe on Big Oak Lane, likely headed to work.

Joe stood from his lawn chair and walked the short distance along Big Oak Lane to Wilshire Lane. He walked carefully, hyperaware of BK in his pocket. He turned left onto Wilshire and stopped in front of the first house on the corner.

The Pratts' brick mansion towered over Joe. He walked up the circular driveway to the front door. The oak door was wide enough for three people and tall enough for an NBA center. He pressed the doorbell, and yippy barks ensued.

Linda Pratt opened the door a crack, just enough for her head to fit. Her blond hair was wet with sweat. "What are you doing here?"

"I have a letter to show you." Joe reached into his back pocket and removed the letter. He held it up, so she could see the beautiful cursive. "Is this Elliot's handwritin'?"

Linda narrowed her eyes at the letter. "No. Why?"

Joe put the letter back in his pocket. "Where was your husband when Colleen was murdered?"

Linda drew back. "My God. You're trying to blame Elliot for what you did?"

"I'm tryin' to find the truth."

Linda glowered at Joe. "You already know. I should call the police."

Joe showed his palms in surrender. "Please. Tell me and I'll leave."

She shook her head. "I don't have to tell you anything, but he was with me."

"Thank you." Joe turned and walked down Wilshire Lane.

Joe stopped at the fourth and last house on the short street—a redbrick McMansion with black shutters, multiple peaks, and a four-car garage. Joe reached into his pocket and touched Baby Kitty, checking on her. Joe walked up the driveway and walkway to the front door. He pressed the doorbell.

Stacy Sellers appeared in the sidelight window. "Go away." Her voice was muffled but audible through the window.

"I need to talk to you for a minute," Joe replied.

"I'd rather not talk to you."

"Please. I have a letter to show you, and then I'll leave. It'll take ten seconds."

Stacy moved from the sidelight window. After a long pause, she opened the door. She had dark hair, dark eyes, and a tan complexion. Joe thought she was Italian, but then again maybe it was the time she spent in the sun, lounging around her pool. "What letter?"

A little girl peered out from behind Stacy. "Who's that man?"

Stacy pivoted to her daughter and said, "Get inside!"

The little girl stepped back but still watched the scene.

Baby Kitty meowed in Joe's sweatshirt pocket.

Stacy faced Joe again, her expression hard. She was around forty and looked like it, with deep laugh lines around her mouth and crow's feet at her eyes. "I want you to leave. Now."

Baby Kitty meowed again.

The little girl stepped forward. "He has a kitty in his pocket."

Joe reached into his pocket, removing Baby Kitty. He addressed the little girl. "Guilty as charged. Would you like to pet her?"

The girl tugged on Stacy's sweatpants. "Can I, Mom? Please. Can I?"

Stacy nodded.

"You have to pet her very carefully because she's just a newborn," Joe said. "Okay?"

"Okay," the girl replied.

Joe knelt and held out Baby Kitty to the little girl.

The girl petted BK lightly. "She's so soft."

After a moment, Stacy said, "That's enough, Gracie."

"Can we get a kitten?"

"Maybe. Go back inside."

Gracie frowned at her mother but went back inside.

Joe put BK back in his pocket.

Stacy stepped onto the front stoop, shutting the door behind her. "You have ten seconds."

In the morning light, Joe saw heavy makeup around Stacy's left eye. He wondered if she was covering up a black eye. Joe removed the letter from his back pocket and held it up for Stacy. "Is this Lucas's handwritin'?"

She glanced at the letter. "No. He's a doctor. You can barely read anything he writes."

"Where was he when my wife was murdered?"

She clenched her jaw. "Leave or I'm calling the police." Stacy went back inside, slamming the door behind her.

Chapter 20: Moving

Joe pulled Colleen's garden cart through Virginia state game lands, with a pack on his back. Baby Kitty lay in her cardboard box, tucked tightly onto the garden cart, along with tools and supplies. It was slow going with the heavy pack and filled garden cart on a narrow game trail. By the time Joe made it to the creek, his shirt was soaked with sweat. He pulled the cart off the trail at the creek, but he couldn't walk along the creek like usual. It was too rocky for the garden cart. So, he had to zigzag around the trees with the cart.

When he finally arrived at the stone cabin, he set his pack inside, his lower back immediately feeling relief. He sat against the outdoor wall and fed BK her kitten-milk replacer. She suckled on the bottle.

"It doesn't look like much, but, with a little elbow grease, we can make it livable," Joe said, cradling the kitten.

After feeding BK, Joe stimulated her anus with a wet cotton pad to help her defecate and urinate. "Good girl," Joe said, catching the feces with the cotton pad. Joe tossed the excrement in the brush and washed the cotton pad in the stream.

Then, he unpacked the tools and supplies. He stocked the coolers in the stone cabin with nonperishable calorie-dense food, like instant oatmeal, granola bars, beef jerky, dried fruit, and nuts. He unfolded the small card table he'd brought on the cart. Then, he set up a charcoal water-filtration system to sit on the table. It was a simple system with two cannisters, capable of holding two gallons of water. The top cannister housed a charcoal filter that purified the water, prior to filling the lower cannister. The lower cannister had a spigot. The creek water appeared clean, but Joe wasn't sure. He filled the upper cannister with creek water. Two hours later, he would have one gallon of clean water.

Once the food and water sources were secure, Joe repaired the roof with some scraps of plywood, asphalt shingles, and roofing nails. He fixed the broken window panes with plywood too. The repairs were done by lunchtime, and Baby Kitty was meowing. Joe stopped to feed BK and to eat something himself.

After lunch, he spent the rest of the day chopping trees and stacking firewood. He set stone along the outside of the house to make a floor for the firewood. Then, he stacked the wood, alternating the stacking direction to maximize airflow. The roof overhang would keep the wood mostly dry in the rain.

At the end of the day, he mixed some kitten-milk replacer with water he'd purified, feeding BK once more, before they returned home. He leaned against the firewood stack, cradling and feeding BK. "I don't know what to think, BK. If she wasn't seein' Lucas or Elliot, then I don't know."

BK suckled, her little white paws with pink pads wrapped around the bottle.

Joe listened to the forest around him. Chickadees called back and forth with their song. Leaves rustled here and there. The running creek water sounded more like a trickle than a *woosh*. "I wanna be angry with her, but I don't feel angry." Joe exhaled. "Disappointed in her maybe, but mostly I'm disappointed in myself. I wasn't the husband I should've been. I have nothin' to show for my life. My daughter hates me, and my wife's dead. I don't know how to live with that."

Chapter 21: Twelve Days Later …

In the grocery store parking lot, Joe loaded nonperishable food and supplies onto the carrier attached to Colleen's bicycle. In the summer, Colleen used to do all the grocery shopping by bicycle. It had been her scheme to stay in shape and to help the environment at the same time.

Baby Kitty was in the backpack on Joe's back. She was walking now and had opened her eyes. The backpack was made as a carrier for kittens, with breathing holes, a little blanket, and a plastic window to watch the world. Joe had paid for the supplies with some of the cash he'd made from the estate sale. Instead of depositing the money into his bank account, he had cashed the check, not wanting his creditors to get their grubby hands on his money.

Nearby, a young man stood by an old minivan, holding a sign that read Please Help. Need Money to Get Home. The minivan had Ontario plates. Joe walked over to the man, with a patchy beard, who wore jeans and a dirty T-shirt.

"Hey. I'm Joe." Joe held out his hand.

The young man shook Joe's hand and replied, "I'm Kurt."

"You're from Canada, huh?"

"Yeah. I lost my job, and I need to get home. My parents won't send me any money. I just need enough for gas and some food for my wife and baby." He gestured to the minivan. "They're in back."

Joe nodded, as he saw the wife in the window. "I could help you out, but I can't give you cash."

His shoulders slumped. "I'll take anything."

"You gotta pen?"

"I think so. Hold on." Kurt went into his minivan to grab a pen.

Joe removed his wallet from his back pocket and took out all his credit cards. Then, he grabbed his cell phone.

Kurt came back from the minivan with a pen and handed it to Joe.

"Thanks," Joe said, taking the pen. He held up his three credit cards. "These credit cards are almost maxed, but there's still a few hundred dollars left on each. I'm gonna call and find out exactly how much. I'll write the amount on the back. Then, you can use the cards to get back to Canada."

Kurt gaped at Joe.

"There's one catch. I'm gonna check with my credit cards to monitor your purchases. If you're not making your way to Ontario, I'll shut off the cards."

Kurt knitted his brow. "I don't know, man. Are those cards stolen?"

"No." Joe removed his license from his wallet and showed Kurt that the name on his license matched his credit cards.

"I don't understand why you're doing this."

"I'm filin' for bankruptcy in a few months. This debt's gonna be wiped anyway. I know this Visa has $320 left on it. I checked a few days ago, and I haven't used it since." Joe wrote 320/22666 on the back of the card, then handed it to Kurt. "On the back I wrote the amount left and my zip code. Go fill up your van. If it works, you know I'm tellin' the truth."

Kurt inspected the card, flipping it over in his hand. "Really?"

"Yeah. Go ahead. Then, come back here, and I'll give you the rest of my cards. While you're fillin' up, I'll call and find out how much is left on the other ones."

Kurt narrowed his eyes at Joe for a moment, then said, "Yeah, okay. Thanks."

Joe called his other credit cards for available balances, while Kurt went to the gas station and filled his minivan. When Kurt came back, his young wife and baby exited the minivan with him.

Kurt approached Joe in the grocery store parking lot, his wife and baby in tow.

"Did the card work okay?" Joe asked.

"Yeah. Thanks, man. I appreciate it," Kurt replied. "We've been stuck here all day. I didn't think we'd ever find help."

Kurt's wife chimed in, cradling a baby in her arms. "Thank you so much, sir."

Joe smiled. "You're both very welcome." Joe handed them his other cards. "Take these too. The amount that you can spend is written on the back."

Kurt nodded.

"Don't forget. Make sure you go home. If you don't, I'm turnin' off these cards."

"We're going straight home," Kurt said, smiling.

"One more thing." Joe removed his cell phone from his pocket. "You want my cell phone?"

Chapter 22: The Auction

The West Clarke County Courthouse had thick concrete pillars in front and concrete steps that spanned the length of the building. Joe stood at the bottom of the steps, his bicycle standing next to him on a kickstand. He wore sunglasses, his hood over his head, and his backpack cat carrier with Baby Kitty inside. A small crowd bustled about the steps. Joe stayed at the edge of the crowd, using various strangers to conceal him from his enemies.

Criers from various banks announced their foreclosures. People made their bids on the steps of the courthouse. Winning bidders were expected to pay immediately with their cashier's checks. Joe wasn't focused on the bank foreclosures though. He was focused on the county attorney—a white-haired man in a dark suit. Elliot Pratt, Fred Nielsen, and Lieutenant Harold Flynn surrounded the county attorney. Harold wasn't wearing his police uniform. Two other men and a heavyset woman were also awaiting the auction for Joe's property.

The attorney announced Joe's property and spent the next several minutes disclosing all the disclaimers and legalese that all the criers offered prior to the bidding. The small crowd came to attention when the attorney said, "The bid starts at $150,000. Do I have $150,000?"

The woman raised her hand.

The attorney pointed to the woman. "I have one-fifty. Do I have one seventy-five?"

Elliot Pratt raised his hand, a scowl on his face.

Joe wondered if Elliot was expecting to bid unopposed.

The attorney pointed at Elliot. "I have one seventy-five. Do I have one eighty-five?"

The woman raised her hand.

The attorney pointed at the woman again. "I have one eighty-five. Do I have two hundred thousand?"

Elliot raised his hand.

The attorney pointed at Elliot. "I have two hundred. Do I have two ten?"

The heavyset woman shook her head.

"Two hundred thousand, going once, going twice, … sold."

Baby Kitty meowed in the backpack.

Fred grinned and shook hands with Harold. Elliot walked away with the county attorney to pay for his new property. The other bidders scattered to the bank auctions, hopeful for a better deal.

Joe mounted his bicycle and drove away, back toward the stone hunting cabin. As he pedaled down the city street, he thought, *This confirms my suspicion. Harold hit me with fines I couldn't afford to get me off the property. Fred will now help Elliot change the zonin' to approve higher-density housin', which makes the property much more valuable than two hundred K. Elliot kicks them both back some cash, then he builds a bunch of town houses or apartments and makes a killin'. And they get me out of the neighborhood as a bonus. Does this have anything to do with Colleen's murder?* Joe stopped his bike at an intersection, waiting for the traffic. *I don't know, but I'm gonna find out.*

Chapter 23: Three Months Later ...

Embers glowed red in the fireplace. A small fire was more than enough to heat the tiny stone cabin. Crates were stacked along one wall, filled with clothes and supplies. The single bed frame now had a mattress, sheets, a thick blanket, and a pillow. A flashlight sat on the card table, shining upward. The batteries had been charged by a solar panel during the day. A handful of Colleen's paintings adorned the walls, including the drawing of the eye with the couple inside the pupil.

Baby Kitty lay on Joe's bed, like a sphinx, her little white paws before her. She watched Joe with greenish-yellow eyes. She was nearly four months old and over four pounds.

Joe paced along the wall opposite the crates. His face was covered by a bushy salt-and-pepper beard, and his hair was wild. The wall was covered in papers filled with stick-figure drawings and Joe's jagged handwriting. A calendar hung on the same wall, black *X*s through the first twenty-seven days of October. "The question is whether or not they killed Colleen to get our property. Maybe they figured, if they killed her and pinned it on me, I'd go to jail, and then they could get our property." Joe held up one finger, making eye contact with BK. "But I had a hung jury ... twice."

Baby Kitty tilted her ears to Joe, her eyes following him, as he paced back and forth.

"They crushed me with code violations. Ran up the fees so high that I lost the house. Or … someone else killed Colleen, and my ex-neighbors were just takin' advantage of her death. If it was someone else, it had to be whoever wrote this letter." Joe pointed to the jilted love letter that hung on the wall. Joe turned to the cat. "What do you think, BK?"

She stared at Joe.

"I know. We've been goin' over this for months. But, if we're gonna make this right, we have to be sure. I need you to go over this with me one more time."

BK still stared at Joe.

"I know we can't bring back Colleen or Patches, but we can punish the ones who hurt them."

BK blinked.

"I know we already know who hurt Patches. Don't worry. We'll get him back."

BK made a noise that sounded like *woo*.

"Soon. I promise. Can we please go over this again? I still feel like I'm missin' somethin' important." Joe paused for an instant. "Thanks." Then, he turned to the five stick-figure drawings on the wall. Joe had drawn T-shirts on each one, with their names scrawled across the shirts. Fred, Lucas, Tera, Elliot, and Harold. Fred, Lucas, and Elliot had short hair. Tera had long hair. And true to life, Harold had no hair. Joe had scrawled notes haphazardly around each stick figure, highlighting all the evidence and speculation pointing to their guilt in regard to Colleen's murder.

Joe slapped Fred's stick figure and turned to BK. "We already know Fred Nielsen's a sick twisted murderer. He killed Patches in cold blood. Maybe he killed Colleen too. He was involved in stealin' our property. What do you think?"

BK blinked again.

"I agree. He's still a maybe." Joe slapped Lucas's stick figure. He had drawn a stethoscope around the doctor's rudimentary portrait. "Lucas

Sellers. I'm pretty sure he beats his wife. Remember when we went to see Stacy? She was wearin' heavy makeup around her eye. This isn't surprisin'. Linda told Colleen that she thought Lucas was abusin' Stacy years ago. Lucas was the one who sexually harassed Colleen. He's a real creep. Maybe Colleen wasn't havin' an affair. Maybe Lucas was just obsessed with her."

BK looked away from Joe.

"You're right. Lucas's handwritin' didn't match the letter, but that was accordin' to Stacy. Maybe she's coverin' for him. She must be scared of him." Joe held out his hands. "What do you think?"

BK yawned.

"We'll keep him as a maybe." Joe slapped the stick figure picture of Tera. Joe had given the figure long hair and bulging muscles on the thighs and biceps for the CrossFit queen and middle school principal. "Tera Hensley-Jones. As far as I know, she wasn't involved in stealin' our property. I doubt she needs the money. Her husband's loaded. Of course, Tera hated Colleen. She did everything she could to make Colleen's job miserable. But Colleen got her back, which is the reason why I think it could've been Tera. Colleen had proof that Tera was havin' an affair with a male gym teacher, and Colleen was gonna tell the school board and her husband if Tera didn't leave Colleen alone. Colleen had heard a rumor about the affair, but she was bluffin' about the proof. It worked though. Tera never bothered her again. No more shit detail at school. No more bad evaluations. Nothin'. It's possible that Tera was still pissed about bein' blackmailed. Whoever killed Colleen did take her laptop and phone. Maybe Tera was worried that Colleen could tell on her at any time, and she didn't want that hangin' over her head."

Joe walked over to the bed and petted BK. "You think she did it?"

BK purred.

"I know. The blackmailin' was over two years before Colleen died.

Why wait that long?" Joe walked back to the stick-figure pictures on the wall. He slapped Elliot's. His stick-figure picture included a little stick-figure dog. "As far as I'm concerned, this piece of shit stole our house. He's the real estate developer with a few million reasons to kill Colleen." Joe turned to BK. "Any thoughts on Elliot?"

BK stood and flopped on her side, showing the white fur on her belly.

"You're ready to take them all down, aren't you?"

BK licked herself.

Joe turned and slapped the bald stick figure. "Lieutenant Harold Flynn. The power-hungry cop. He was involved in stealin' our house. He would know how to cover up a murder." Joe walked over to the bed and sat.

Baby Kitty stepped into Joe's lap and lay in a circle.

"I don't know if we'll ever figure out who killed Colleen, but every one of 'em is guilty of somethin'. I think it's time to make 'em pay."

BK purred.

Joe glanced at the calendar on the wall. "Tomorrow's Saturday. Maybe we should crash the Pratts' party."

Chapter 24: Reconnaissance

Joe hiked through the woods, the beam of his flashlight illuminating the game trail. He wore all black and the backpack cat carrier, with BK inside.

After an hour of hiking, Joe stopped at the edge of the Virginia state game lands, peering into what was once his house and property. Joe gasped at the construction site. It had been three months since he'd been there. His old saltbox house was gone. Much of the forest that covered his six acres had been clear-cut. Gravel roads had been installed, allowing access to town houses in various stages of completion. Some were still weedy plots, marked with stakes. Some were holes in the ground, awaiting concrete for the basements. Others had basements and two-story wooden skeletons, awaiting particle board and cheap siding. One row of five townhomes appeared nearly complete. A banner hanging from the model home read Townhomes at Wilshire Commons, From the 190s.

Joe shook his head. "They say this is progress."

Baby Kitty meowed.

Joe stepped through the raspberry brambles, the thorns tugging on his pants. He walked through the construction site. Yellow construction equipment sat idle around the future town house community. Stacks of two-by-fours and particle board were strategically placed near those town houses that were ready for their bones.

Faint laughter carried to Joe, coming from the Pratts' house. Joe followed the laughter and the light coming from their backyard. Joe crept through the dark, stopping at the six-foot-tall privacy fence surrounding the Pratts' backyard. He stood on his tippy toes and peered over the fence.

A flagstone patio was connected to the back of the house. A gas grill stood on one end of the patio; a hot tub stood on the other end. Faux tiki torches with LED lights surrounded the patio, illuminating Joe's ex-neighbors, who sat around the patio table. Elliot Pratt, Lucas Sellers, and Fred Nielsen sat at one end of the table, drinking their beer and talking. The wives—Linda, Stacy, and Joan—sat at the other end of the table, drinking their wine. Unsurprisingly, Tera and her geriatric husband weren't there. Linda had stopped inviting them years ago, siding with Colleen, during their conflict over the expulsion of Justin Franks.

Joe took off his backpack and sat on the ground, his back against the fence, obscured by an arborvitae hedge. He let Baby Kitty out of the backpack cat carrier. She stepped into Joe's lap, kneading his thigh with her front paws, before laying in a circle. Joe petted BK, while he listened to two conversations simultaneously.

"You must be so excited about your vacation," Joan Nielsen said.

"It'll be nice to get away," Linda replied. "Elliot's been so busy with Wilshire Commons."

"Are you taking Bianca?"

"No. I'm taking her to the kennel on Monday morning, before we go to the airport."

The men talked about Lucas's new Porsche.

"It looks exactly like your old Porsche," Fred said.

"It's a totally different car," Lucas replied. "My old car was a 911 Carrera. This one's a 911 GT3. It's basically a race car for the street. Five hundred horsepower from a four liter, flat six. It does the quarter mile in 11.2 seconds and has a top speed of 202 miles per hour."

Elliot let out a low whistle. "I'd have my license taken in a week."

"How much did it set you back?" Fred asked.

"One seventy," Lucas replied.

Someone spat their beer.

"One seventy! A hundred and seventy grand?" Fred asked.

Bianca barked, causing Baby Kitty to bolt toward the Nielsens' house next door.

Shit.

Bianca galloped toward the fence, still barking.

"What's her problem?" Elliot asked.

"I'll get her," Linda replied.

Joe crept away from the scene, following BK.

Chapter 25: It's Always the Husband

Joe found Baby Kitty hiding under the bushes alongside Fred's garage. Joe bent down and held out his hand. "It's all right, BK. You can come out now."

BK meowed and stepped to Joe, rubbing her head against his hand.

Joe petted her. "This is the house of the man who murdered your mother. Maybe we should kill what he loves the most. What do you think?"

BK purred.

"I agree. It's time."

Joe stood and went to the people-size door alongside the garage. The top half of the door had a window with multiple square glass panes. He jabbed the lower right pane, just hard enough to crack the glass, his fist protected by his leather glove. Then, he pushed on the cracked glass— shards of glass falling into the garage—creating a hole big enough for his hand. Joe reached through the hole and unlocked the door.

BK meowed.

Joe bent over and scooped her up, cradling her in one arm. He opened the door and stepped into the garage, shutting the door behind him. Glass shards crackled under his boots. He flipped on his flashlight, scanning the space.

A Ford sedan, a Ford SUV, and a zero-turn mower were parked in the three-car garage. The vehicles and the mower were showroom clean.

Joe kicked the glass shards under the nearby workbench. Tools hung on a pegboard. A free-standing toolbox, fit for a professional mechanic, stood next to the workbench. Baby Kitty wriggled from Joe's grasp and jumped to the concrete floor. She sauntered over to the spotless sedan, leaped on the car, and walked across the hood, leaving paw prints.

Joe walked alongside the sedan toward the back wall. The wall contained an elaborate irrigation control box, with PVC piping, a valve box, injectors, and a fertilizer tank. At least Joe assumed it was a fertilizer tank. It was half full with a bluish liquid. A gallon jug of concentrated fertilizer sat next to the tank. *This is a fertigation system.* Fertigation allowed for fertilizer and pesticides to be spread by the irrigation system. Joe used to haul livestock and hay for several farmers in the area. One of them had been growing vegetables with a fertigation system. It was much bigger and a drip system, but the plumbing appeared similar. *This would be easy to break.* Joe walked beyond the irrigation setup, inspecting the garden tools, all hanging from hooks on the back wall. Not a speck of dirt was on the shiny shovels and rakes.

He moved to the wall connected to the house and tried to open the door, but it was locked. *I could kick it in. Then what? What he loves isn't inside.* Joe browsed the metal shelves next to the door. They held garden supplies and car wash chemicals and neatly stacked crates filled with odds and ends. Joe inspected the two-and-a-half-gallon jug of Roundup Pro concentrate. He grabbed the heavy jug from the shelf and lugged it back to the irrigation setup.

Joe opened the fertilizer tank and grinned, as he dumped much of the Roundup concentrate inside. "This is for you, Patches." Then, he put the Roundup jug back on the metal shelf. He searched the garage with his flashlight. "BK. Where are you?"

Baby Kitty meowed and stood from the seat on the zero-turn mower.

Joe walked over to BK. He petted her and said, "It's done. What

Fred loves the most will soon be dead."

BK rubbed her head against Joe's hand.

"We should go, before we get caught. They'll send me to jail, and you'll be sent to a shelter. You don't wanna know what happens at the shelter."

Joe put BK back inside the backpack cat carrier and shouldered the pack. He left the garage, locking the door handle, and shutting the door on his way out. He walked next door, behind Tera and Randall's house. Light came from the first floor.

Tera and Randall's McMansion was a stone-faced colonial, with a three-car garage and a privacy fence surrounding the backyard. Joe tried to open the back gate, but it was locked. He stood on his tippy toes, checking the backyard and the house. An ADT Security sign stood in front of the back patio. Light came from the first floor of the house, but the windows were covered with blinds.

Joe crept around to the front of the house, crouching, and hiding behind the front boxwood hedges. Another ADT sign stood in the front flower bed. He raised his head just enough to peek into the front bay window. The curtains were drawn but not completely. Through the sliver between the curtains, Joe had a small view of the open-concept living room, decorated with white-and-silver furniture, oriental area rugs, and a glass coffee table. Beyond the living room, Tera sat at the dining room table, eating and tapping her phone. Joe stood up taller to get a better view.

His head triggered the motion light, bathing Joe in bright light. He ran from the bushes back to the rear of the property, hiding against the privacy fence. He waited for several minutes but didn't hear anything untoward.

Joe walked behind the last house on Wilshire Lane. The Sellers's pool was lit from below, giving it an eerie green glow. The surface of the water was as smooth as glass in the still night. Lights were on throughout the house. Joe wondered if they had a babysitter or if they left their kids alone, while they partied down the street.

Joe crept through the backyard to the garage alongside the house. No easy access door, like at Fred's house. No easy way in. The four-car garage, like the rest of the house, was brick. No siding whatsoever. Joe thought about what Lucas had said to Colleen. *Was that the first time he said somethin' like that to her?* He imagined Lucas with his hands around Colleen's neck. He thought about destroying what Lucas loved the most, so he could feel like Joe felt. *I need access to his Porsche.*

Approaching voices came from the street.

Joe snuck to the front corner of the garage and peered in the direction of the voices. Lucas Sellers pulled Stacy by the wrist.

"Let go of me," Stacy said, struggling against her husband.

Lucas turned around and backhanded her, knocking her to the asphalt.

She yelped and held her hand to her cheek, not attempting to rise from her seated position. "I'm done with you. *Done!*"

Lucas stood over her and pointed in her face. "You're done when I say you're done. And if you ever embarrass me like that again …"

"What? What are you gonna do?"

Lucas glared at his wife, speechless.

Stacy stood from the asphalt and wiped off her pants. She held out her hands. "What are you gonna do? Kill me?"

Chapter 26: Max Flow

An owl hooted from a nearby tree. Joe put on his gloves and tried to open the Pratts' back gate, but it was locked. He stood on his tippy toes and peered over the privacy fence. The house was dark, except for the exterior lighting. The Pratts were likely on their vacation, as Joe had overheard two nights earlier. Joe removed his cat carrier backpack, setting it and Baby Kitty on the ground. He looked through the plastic window at BK and said, "I'll be right back."

Joe climbed over the privacy fence, then unlocked and opened the back gate. He grabbed the cat carrier backpack and walked to the stone patio. BK scratched at the cat carrier and whined, eager to be released. Joe set down the backpack and let out BK.

She rubbed against Joe's calf.

"It looks like they're gone," Joe said. "I don't know if they have an alarm system. They don't advertise it, like Tera does. If they do, hopefully they don't have motion sensors."

He walked to the back door and knelt in front of Bianca's doggy door. Joe pushed open the small door, peering inside. The doggy door led to the kitchen. To the right of the kitchen was a family room, with a stone fireplace, a flat-screen television, and leather couches. Baby Kitty bolted inside.

"BK. Get back here," Joe said in a hushed whisper. He worried that she might trigger a motion sensor.

BK turned back to Joe.

"BK. Get back here."

BK walked deeper into the house, sniffing as she went.

"Damn it." *Maybe they don't have motion alarms. I wouldn't with a dog in the house.*

Joe waited for a few minutes, expecting the alarm to blare, but it was still quiet. He stood and searched along the back of the house for the spigot. He found the spigot and a rolled-up hose near the left corner of the house. He removed the pistol-grip nozzle from the hose end. Then, he pulled the hose to the back door. Joe shoved the hose end through the doggy door, pushing it as far in as he could, which wasn't very far. *What if the floor's tilted toward the door? Then the water would seep under the door and back outside. The damage would be minimal.* Joe looked around for something to push the hose end deeper inside. He walked over to the covered hot tub. A short pool skimmer leaned against the hot tub. Joe picked it up, inspecting the pole. *It's extendable.* Joe pressed the button on the pole and pulled it, turning the six-foot pole into a ten-foot pole.

Joe went back to the doggy door. He shoved the blunt end of the pole into the doggy door and pushed the hose end deeper into the Pratts' mansion. He returned the pole to its original length and location.

Then, he went back to the spigot and placed his gloved hand on the handle. "This one's for me." He turned the water on full blast and grinned.

Joe walked back to the doggy door again. No water came from the hose end … yet. He bent down and opened the doggy door, sticking his face in the opening. "BK. Come here. Let's go." She didn't come, which was unlike her, although she was getting more independent as she aged.

Water spurted from the hose end. Then, it came out steadily, the water spreading across the hardwood. The water didn't come back to the door, as Joe had worried. It spread in multiple directions, like a pond ripple. Some of the water slipped under a door that Joe knew was the staircase to the Pratts' precious party basement. He envisioned the water seeping downstairs and ruining anything and everything it touched with future mold.

BK jumped off the kitchen counter and came into view. She hissed at the water and ran through the doggy door. Joe smiled and picked up BK, placing her back into the cat carrier.

Joe hiked back to the stone cabin, with BK in the carrier on his back, his flashlight illuminating the game trail. "How long do you think they'll be gone?" Joe paused for a beat. "We know they left today. People who take an airplane on vacation are usually gone for at least a week. Let's say it's a week. That hose has to be putting out at least two gallons per minute. That's 120 gallons per hour. That's 2,400 gallons for twenty hours. Add another 480, gives you 2880 per day. Let's call it three thousand to make the math easy. That would be 21,000 gallons of water in their house!" Joe cackled in the moonlight, thinking about destroying the thing that Elliot loved the most.

Chapter 27: Nice Ride

Two days later, Joe trekked back to Wilshire Lane before sunrise. BK rode on his back in her carrier. His breath condensed in the air, as he walked through the dormant construction site.

Joe stopped by the Pratts' mansion and peered over the privacy fence. It appeared that the water was still running, although he saw no outward evidence of the destruction inside. Joe walked by Fred and Joan's house. The lawn and landscape was still pristine—no evidence of the poison Joe had added to the fertigation tank.

He knew Roundup took a week or so to take effect, depending on the temperature and the sunlight. *What if Fred's not irrigatin' anymore for the season? It was October 28th when I put Roundup in the fertilizer tank. If he irrigated the next day, that would be three days ago. I wouldn't water my lawn in November. But he still had fertilizer in the tank. I doubt he would leave that over the winter. It probably has to be cleaned out every year.*

Joe continued walking along the backyards. Tera's house was dark, except for a few outdoor lights. Same with the Sellers's house. Joe found a good place at the edge of the state game lands to hide and to spy on Lucas and Tera. Joe sat against an oak, wearing camouflaged hunting gear. BK meowed and scratched at the inside of her carrier. Joe let her out of the cat carrier. She dug in the leaves, squatted, and peed, then covered the evidence. Joe watched the houses through his binoculars. He had to pee too, but he was saving that for later.

***

Lucas Sellers was the first to leave in his BMW at 6:34 a.m. Tera Hensley-Jones left in her Mercedes convertible at 7:02 a.m. By this time, the construction site was bustling with activity, the hum of diesel engines in the air. Joe wondered about Randall. Not that Joe had been looking for him, but Joe hadn't seen Randall in a long time. *I wonder if he died. He was pretty old the last time I saw him. When was that? It was at a Pratt party. Before Justin Franks was expelled.* Joe rubbed his bushy beard, thinking. *It had to be at least four or five years ago.*

An upstairs light came on at the Sellers's house. *Time to get ready for school.* Joe knew from Colleen that the elementary kids started school an hour later than the middle school kids. Colleen used to complain about the early morning starts, often lamenting that she wished that they started at the same time as the elementary schools. The staggered start was necessary though because they didn't have enough buses for all the students in the West Clarke County School District to begin at the same time. Joe knew that Stacy and Lucas had two children in elementary school. Joe was banking on Stacy being the type of mother who drove her children to school.

Joe stood and scanned the area for Baby Kitty. He grabbed her cat treats from his pocket, shook it, and said, "BK. Come here, BK."

She galloped toward him, jumping over branches and tree roots.

Joe bent down and scooped her up. "Good girl." Joe put her back in the carrier, with a handful of cat treats, and crept down to the Sellers's house. He walked past the pool and crept alongside the garage, situated on the left side of the house, facing the side lawn. He waited at the corner of the garage, hoping that he was right about her.

A half-hour later, voices came from the garage, followed by the opening and shutting of car doors. The garage-door opener rumbled, and the door nearest Joe lifted. A BMW SUV backed out of the garage, stopping at the edge of the asphalt driveway. Stacy pressed the garage door opener on her visor. The garage door rumbled down. Stacy turned the wheel of her SUV and drove down the driveway toward Wilshire Lane. Joe crept around the garage and stuck his foot under the nearly shut garage door, triggering the safety. The garage door lifted again. Joe glanced down the driveway at Wilshire Lane. Stacy's SUV was already gone, likely headed for school.

Joe entered the garage. He went to the garage door console, wearing his leather gloves, and pressed the button. The garage door motored down again, giving him the privacy he needed. BK meowed and scratched at her cat carrier again. Joe took off his backpack and released BK. "I can't keep takin' you, if you can't be quiet."

BK sniffed the air, then set about exploring.

Joe surveyed the four-car garage. The left-hand space was crammed with junk—old exercise equipment, furniture, and cardboard boxes filled with all the things that a wealthy family of four accumulated over the years. Joe turned his attention to the black Porsche GT3 parked next to the junk space. He approached the sparkling race car for the street. Joe wasn't a car guy, but he admired the flared fenders, wide tires, and massive brakes.

Baby Kitty jumped on the hood, her dirty feet leaving paw prints.

Joe smiled at her. "Doesn't seem so special to you, huh?"

She meowed and walked up the windshield to the roof.

Joe removed the knife attached to the scabbard on his belt. "You want me to sign it for you?"

BK surveyed the garage from the roof of the Porsche.

Joe used his knife to carve a circle the size of a large pizza into the hood. BK watched Joe work from the roof of the Porsche. Joe added kitty ears, a smiley mouth, and whiskers, carving through the paint down to the metal. He finished his masterpiece with a jagged message. *Nice ride!* He signed it, *Baby Kitty.*

"What do you think?" Joe asked, eyeing BK.

She sat on the roof, licking herself.

He laughed. "I know. It's funny, right?"

BK stood and walked back down the windshield to the hood. Then, she hopped off the hood and sniffed around the junk.

Joe checked the junk, searching for a plastic container. He found a bucket. Joe reached into his camo pants and removed a large Ziploc bag from a cargo pocket. Inside, was a pound of cat shit. He opened the bag, keeping his nose back. Despite not getting a direct whiff, the putrid smell made him gag. Joe dumped the contents into the bucket. Then, he resealed the Ziploc bag, putting it back into his pocket, not wanting to leave any evidence. Joe looked around, unzipped his pants, and pulled out his penis. Steam rose from the bucket as he peed into it. The smell of ammonia mixed with the smell of cat shit. It was a lot of urine, as Joe had been holding it specifically for this purpose.

Joe put his penis back into his pants and zipped up. Then, he found a wiffle-ball bat. He lifted his shirt collar over his nose and used the end of the bat to mash the cat shit and to stir the concoction into a slurry. Finally, he took the slurry to the Porsche.

Joe spoke to the car, as if it were Lucas. "This is for Colleen, you piece of shit." Then, he poured the concoction into the air intake vent, just below the windshield. This air intake connected to the vehicle's heating and air-conditioning.

The right-hand garage door rumbled upward.

Shit. Joe ran behind the junk pile, crouching behind a stack of cardboard boxes. "BK. Come here," Joe said in a hushed whisper. But Baby Kitty didn't come. Joe removed the cat treats from his pocket and shook the bag, but she still didn't come.

Stacy and her SUV drove into the garage. She parked and cut the engine. Her door opened and shut. Then, she said in a baby voice, "How did you get in here?"

BK meowed.

"Aww. Aren't you the sweetest little thing?" Stacy said.

Dust from the junk filtered into Joe's nose. He stifled a sneeze.

"I'll leave the garage door open, so you can go home. I hope you have a home." Stacy walked toward the door to the house, closer to Joe, who still hid behind the cardboard boxes. "What's that smell?" Stacy walked over to the Porsche. "Oh my God. Who did this?"

Joe thought she must've noticed his artwork.

"Hello? Is anyone in here?"

Joe sneezed involuntarily.

Stacy screamed and ran back to her SUV. She started her car and reversed wildly out of the garage, raking the side of her vehicle against the garage in the process. Then, she was gone.

Joe emerged from his hiding spot, searching for BK. He shook the cat treats again and said, "BK. BK. Come here."

BK appeared from under an old sofa.

"What were you doin'?" Joe asked.

BK made a noise that sounded like *woo*.

"You're too nice. You're gonna get us caught. Let's get out of here, before the police come."

Chapter 28: I'm Right Here

Three days later, Joe returned to Wilshire Lane, eager to check the Pratts' house and the Nielsens' lawn. Wearing all black and under the cover of darkness, he cut through the construction site. BK was at the stone cabin. After the debacle with Stacy, Joe had decided it was best to leave her at home.

Joe crept behind the Pratts' mansion. Lights were on throughout the house. Windows were open. The hum of industrial fans came from the house. *They won't be able to get rid of the mold. They'll have to strip that house to the bones.*

Joe snuck along the Pratts' privacy fence to the corner to check the Nielsens' house next door. The landscape lighting revealed a straw-brown lawn, dead flowers, and hedges burned black by the poison. Joe smirked to himself.

Then, he spotted a police car parked along Wilshire Lane, between the two McMansions. He moved back behind the privacy fence, sitting and hiding between the fence and the arborvitae hedge.

***

Joe sat there for several hours, waiting and wondering if the neighbors would gather on Saturday night like usual. He was about to leave, when they did, in fact, gather on the Pratts' back patio. But it wasn't a joyous affair, with alcoholic beverages, food, and laughter.

Elliot Pratt started the outdoor propane heater, and the neighbors huddled around the patio table, wearing their jackets. Joe listened, from his spot against the fence.

"It has to be Joe," Fred Nielsen said. "I killed that feral cat he was feeding."

"Why did you do that?" Linda Pratt asked, her tone accusatory.

"It was shitting in my mulch and pissing on my flowers."

"So what?"

"I have every right to defend my home from vermin," Fred said.

"You killed his pet!"

"This isn't helpful," Elliot Pratt said. "It can't be Joe. Detective Green already said—"

"I don't care what he said. He's wrong," Fred replied.

"The last place he used his phone was in Ontario," Linda said.

"That was almost two months ago. I think he's back. He killed my lawn because I killed his cat. I think he flooded your house because he thinks you stole his."

"We didn't steal his house."

"Joe may view it differently. It's him. I know it. Last time I saw him, he seemed crazy."

"There's one big problem with your theory," Elliot said. "If it is Joe, how does Lucas fit into this? What did *you* do to Joe?"

Lucas Sellers hesitated for a beat. "Nothing as far as I know."

Joe clenched his jaw. *You do know. You know exactly what you did.*

"What if he tries to kill us?" Stacy Sellers asked.

"That's what the police are for," Elliot replied. "If it was Joe, I bet he's long gone by now."

"What about Tera?" Linda asked. "She was pretty pissed when I stopped inviting her to our get-togethers. I still think she poisoned Dolly."

Joe remembered Colleen mentioning this years ago. A few months after Linda had taken Colleen's side in the fight over Justin Franks's suspension, Linda's springer spaniel Dolly had died. Linda had had an autopsy done by the vet. The cause of death was ingesting antifreeze. It had been summer when Dolly had died, and Linda had often put Dolly's food and water on the back patio. They never found evidence of the culprit.

"How long ago was that?" Fred asked. "Four years? Longer?"

"She's a grudge holder and a vindictive bitch," Linda replied.

Joe imagined Tera with her hands around Colleen's neck.

"Why would she wait four years and then kill my lawn, destroy Lucas's car, and flood your house?" Fred asked. "All because of a party invitation? I don't buy it. She has her hands full with Randall. I hear he's not in good health."

"I bet she's just waiting for him to die, so she can get his money," Linda said. "You don't marry a man twenty-five years older than you for love."

"She may be a bitch, but she's no gold digger. The money's all going to Randall's daughters."

"We shouldn't be playing detective," Elliot said. "We need to let the police sort this out. In the meantime, we have to be hypervigilant. Whoever it is, they're still out there."

Joe grinned and stroked his bushy beard. *Damn straight. I'm right here.*

Chapter 29: Revelation

Leaves crunched under his boots, as Joe hiked back to the stone cabin, his flashlight leading the way. He went off trail at the creek, following the water until he neared the cabin. Then, he climbed uphill to his home. Baby Kitty stood from the bed and meowed when Joe entered the stone cabin.

"Hey, BK." He shut and locked the door behind him. Then, he set the flashlight on the table, facing the ceiling. Joe petted Baby Kitty, although every day she looked less and less like a baby. "Did you miss me?"

BK rubbed against his hand, meowing.

"I have good news. Fred's yard is dead. We did it."

BK purred.

"I knew you'd be happy. The Pratts are back. They're tryin' to dry out their house, but I think it's ruined. They're gonna have to gut that house." Joe continued to pet BK. "Lucas didn't wanna admit what he did to Colleen. He said he didn't know why he was targeted. What a bunch of bullshit."

BK hopped off the bed and went to the crates along the wall. She turned back to Joe and meowed.

Joe followed her. "You hungry?"

BK answered with a long meow.

"Lemme make a fire first. Then, I'll make dinner." Joe made a fire in the fireplace.

BK watched the fire, mesmerized by the dancing flames.

Joe opened one of the coolers submerged in the ground as makeshift root cellars. He grabbed two pawpaws that he'd foraged recently. Then, he went to the crates along the wall for BK's dried cat food and Joe's oatmeal and beef jerky. Joe had stockpiled enough food to get them through the fall and winter. They would have to ration their stores and then supplement their diet, with hunting and foraging.

BK purred and rubbed against him.

Joe prepared the cat food first, so BK wouldn't whine. He set her plate on the table across from Joe. While BK ate her food, Joe heated a pot of water on the fire. While he waited for the water, he sliced the pawpaws in half and spooned out the custard-like fruit. "Man, I love these. You're missin' out."

BK crunched her dried cat food.

Joe swallowed the fruit. "They were talkin' about somethin' I forgot about. Linda thinks Tera poisoned her old dog. That got me thinkin' about whether or not Tera could've killed Colleen." Joe finished the pawpaws. Then, he opened his beef jerky.

BK left her food to get a bite.

Joe held his beef jerky away from her. "This is mine. You have your food."

"*Woo,*" BK replied.

"Fine." Joe bit off a piece and tossed it in her bowl.

BK gnawed on the beef jerky.

"I still feel like I'm missin' somethin' important. The affair has to be the missin' piece. I need to know who wrote that letter." Joe chewed on the beef jerky, thinking about the letter and that artwork of Colleen's, with the eye. At first, he had thought the picture showed Colleen pushing Joe away. *Maybe it's not me. Maybe it's Colleen pushin' away whoever wrote that jilted love letter.* Joe put the last bit of beef jerky in BK's bowl. Then, he went to the fire and grabbed his pot of boiling water.

Back at the table, Joe poured the water on his oatmeal. "Be careful. This is hot."

BK still chewed her beef jerky.

Joe stirred his oatmeal with a spoon and went to his investigation wall, his bowl in hand. He read the jilted love letter again, noting the beautiful cursive, which was the polar opposite to Joe's jagged chicken scratch. *Is that what you wanted? The opposite of me?* Then, he went to Colleen's drawing of the crying eye, with the silhouette of an estranged couple inside the pupil. It appeared as if one person was holding the other at arm's length—or maybe pushing them away. Shadows from the fire danced around the pupil, highlighting the couple. Joe stared at the silhouette for a long time, almost hypnotized. Then, it hit him like a bolt of lightning.

"Holy shit." Joe turned to BK. "I can't believe I didn't see it." Joe pointed to the drawing. "Look at this, BK."

Baby Kitty stared at Joe.

"The couple inside the eye. They both look similar. I think they're both women." Joe went to the note. "And look at the note. Look at the nice cursive. Looks female. I think Colleen was havin' an affair with a woman." He immediately thought of Linda.

Chapter 30: The Mistress

On Monday morning, Joe hid behind the Pratts' privacy fence, concealed by their arborvitae hedge. His breath condensed in the cool air. He had periodically popped his head over the fence, checking the activity in and around the house. Elliot had already left for work, but he didn't leave until his construction crew had arrived.

Joe stood on his tippy toes and peered over the fence, checking the house again. The construction crew worked inside. Linda shut the curtains in her upstairs bedroom.

This might be my only chance.

Joe walked around to the front door. A roll-off Dumpster was on the driveway, partially filled with moldy drywall and carpet. Joe wore tan cargo pants and a black fleece, purposely not dressed in all black or camo, as he had been on previous missions. He had trimmed his bushy beard and had cut his hair too, hoping to look respectable.

The front door was propped open. Workmen moved in and out, like ants, pushing wheelbarrows filled with moldy drywall. Joe walked through the open door, without anyone saying a word to him. Of course, the workmen couldn't see the Berretta 9mm handgun or the knife concealed by his fleece.

The first-floor furniture had already been removed. Carpet was cut and rolled up and stacked along the walls for removal. Workers removed drywall, exposing the studs. It smelled like mold and mildew.

Black spots crept up the walls, where the drywall still hung.

He proceeded up the stairs, as if he belonged. He walked to the end of the hall to the master bedroom. The upstairs was largely intact. He opened one of the double doors and slipped inside the Pratts' bedroom. Bianca, Linda's prize poodle, sat just inside.

The dog barked.

Joe rushed past the dog and the king-size bed toward the walk-in closets. The dog followed, still barking. Joe opened Linda's closet and went inside. The dog followed, and Joe rushed back out, shutting the dog in the closet. He knew Bianca was all bark and no bite. Joe walked through the connected sitting area, with a gas fireplace, a love seat, and an antique chair.

The *whoosh* of water came from the open bathroom door. Joe retrieved his handgun from his holster and waited next to the door, hidden tight to the wall.

The water stopped. A few minutes later, Linda exited the bathroom wearing a cotton robe. Joe let her walk past him. He grabbed her from behind, putting his left hand over her mouth, and the barrel of his handgun into her back.

Her shriek was muffled by his hand.

Joe said, "Shut up, or I'll kill you."

Her body trembled with fear.

"I'm gonna take my hand off your mouth, but, if you scream, I'll blow your fuckin' head off. You understand?"

She nodded.

Muffled barking came from Linda's walk-in closet.

Joe removed his hand and she turned around to face him.

Her face was red from the shower and the shock. "What do you want?"

"You were havin' an affair with Colleen, weren't you?"

Linda broke eye contact. "I don't know what you're talking about."

Joe pointed his gun in her face and spoke through gritted teeth. "Tell the truth."

She showed her palms reflexively. "Yes, okay! We had an affair. I loved her." Then she whispered, "I still do."

Joe gripped the gun, his knuckles white. "You killed her, didn't you?"

She tilted her head, her brow furrowed. "*No.* I would never. I was devastated. I still am. Please put down the gun."

"That note I showed you. It was yours. Wasn't it?"

Linda's hands trembled. "Yes, but she didn't want me. She wanted *you*. I don't know why. Please put down the gun."

Joe held the gun steady. "If you didn't kill her, it had to be your husband."

"Elliot never did anything to Colleen."

The vein in Joe's neck bulged. "You think I'm stupid, don't you?"

"I don't know what you're talking about—"

"My house. I saw Elliot at the auction with Fred and Harold. They fucked me with all those bullshit code violations, so they could steal my property. Didn't they?"

Linda opened her mouth to speak, but nothing came out.

"But they had to get rid of Colleen and pin her murder on me first." Joe moved closer and pressed the barrel of his gun to Linda's forehead. "*Didn't* they?"

Tears welled in Linda's eyes. Her voice trembled. "It wasn't like that. Everyone loved Colleen. After the trial, everyone was scared to live next to you. That's why they started calling Harold." She blinked, and tears slipped down her face. "Please, Joe. Don't do this. I loved Colleen more than life itself. I miss her every day."

Joe stared at her for a long moment. Then, he lowered his gun. "If you wanna live, you'll do exactly as I say."

Linda nodded, her face tear-streaked.

Joe prodded her to the antique chair in the sitting area. "Take that chair and put it in Elliot's closet."

She grabbed the chair and carried it to Elliot's walk-in closet, which was filled with tailored suits, ties, and shiny shoes.

Bianca's muffled barking played in the background.

Joe gestured to the chair with his handgun. "Sit."

Linda sat.

Joe set his handgun just outside the closet behind them, far out of reach. He turned back to Linda.

She looked past him to the gun on the carpet.

"Don't even think about it," he said. "You won't get past me. If you try, I'll kill you. Understand me?"

Linda nodded again.

Joe retrieved a roll of duct tape from his cargo pants. He taped her hands together and her ankles to the chair.

Linda didn't move as he worked. "You don't have to do this."

Joe ran tape around the chair and her bare calves. "How do you know what I have to do?"

"We can work it out. I can get you a lawyer. We can figure out what happened to Colleen together."

"Shut up." Joe pulled the tape around her waist, fastening her to the chair.

"Please. I want what you want."

Joe slapped a piece of tape over her mouth. "I'm done talkin' to you."

Linda tried to talk, but it came out as muffled grunts.

He used the rest of the roll, taping her torso—just below her breasts—to the chair. Joe stood and inspected his tape job. *That'll hold for a few hours.*

Linda grunted, trying to talk.

He placed his finger under her chin, raising her gaze to meet his. "If

I find out you killed Colleen, I *will* kill you. Same goes for your piece of shit husband."

Joe left the closet, shutting the door behind him. He grabbed his gun from the floor and holstered it. Then, he pulled the love seat from the sitting area, setting it in front of the closet door, barricading Linda inside.

Chapter 31: Dirt

Joe slipped out the back door to the Pratts' patio. He walked through the grass and through the back gate. Then, he followed the privacy fence and crouched near the corner, obscured by the arborvitae hedge. He had imagined scaring a confession out of Linda, but her denials were believable.

Now what? If it wasn't Linda, and my property had nothin' to do with it, then who? Lucas? Tera? A random act of violence? A burglary gone wrong? They did take her computer and phone. I need to make a decision quick. Someone will find Linda soon. He stroked his beard, thinking for a moment. *Tera's the last one on my hit list. If I don't hit her house now, I may not be able to do it later.*

Joe peered around the corner of the fence, spotting the police car on Wilshire Lane, parked between the Pratts' and the Nielsens'. The officer stared down at something. *Probably his phone.* Joe cut through the backyards, fast-walking through the Nielsens' lawn to Tera's backyard and privacy fence. He walked around the fence to the side of the house and the garage. He gazed into the garage window. Tera's Mercedes convertible was gone, but a Mercedes SUV was parked inside. *Randall might be home.*

He returned to the backyard, scaled the privacy fence, and walked to the rear of the house. An ADT sign warned would-be burglars. Joe peered into the windows, checking for Randall and any motion

88

detectors mounted on the wall corners. Joe's old security system had motion detectors on the first floor. The techs had installed them in the corners, about eight feet up the walls. No sign of Randall and no motion detectors, from Joe's perspective.

He inspected the windows, noticing the contacts. If he opened a window, that would trigger the alarm. *If she has contacts on the windows, it's guaranteed that she has contacts on the doors.* Joe removed his handgun from his holster. The *hum* of the diesel engines came from the construction site, along with the *pop* of a nail gun. He picked a window that wasn't easily visible from outside of the privacy fence. Joe broke the glass in several places with the butt of his gun. He stopped and listened for any movement in the house.

After a minute of listening, he holstered his weapon. *Maybe Randall's in a nursing home.* Joe wore his leather gloves to remove the remaining glass still stuck to the panes. Then, instead of unlocking and opening the window, he removed the flimsy grid that had been holding the glass and crawled inside. The contacts on the window were still in place. As far as the alarm system knew, the window remained shut.

He stood and brushed the glass shards off his pants. The family room featured a brown leather sectional, a wall-mounted flat screen, and a stone fireplace. Dirty dishes sat on the wooden coffee table. Workout clothes were strewn about the couch. Joe walked through the kitchen to the dining room. A long wooden table was covered by a food-stained linen tablecloth. Hutches stood along opposing walls, featuring antique china and silverware. A few dirty plates littered the table. *I didn't know they were such slobs. I'm surprised they don't have a maid.*

Joe left the dining room for the living room. Elegant white couches paired with a glass coffee table and a white Oriental rug created an elegant sitting area. No dirty plates, but he saw a thick sheet of dust. Joe scanned the area beyond, spotting the office, then walked that way.

A mammoth wooden desk dominated the office. Bookshelves lined one wall, along with a filing cabinet. A laptop sat on the desk, along with mail and bills in haphazard piles. Several books were also on the desktop and the nearby leather couch. *Dark Psychology, Mindfulness and the Art of Mind Control, The Science of Thought Control, Brainwashing Techniques, The Art of Persuasion*, and *Mind Programming*.

Joe went through the desk drawers, unsure of what he was searching for. The drawers were filled with school supplies. Boxes of pens, pencils, staples, paper, notebooks, folders, and paper clips. Many of the boxes were labeled WCCSD, which stood for West Clarke County School District.

Then, he went to the filing cabinet and opened the top drawer, inspecting the hanging file folders. It was filled with manuals and warranties for various household appliances and electronics. Joe shut the metal drawer and opened the next drawer down. Ten years of tax returns were inside, along with insurance documents, bank statements, and a Last Will and Testament. Joe grabbed the will from the file folder. A small USB flash drive was clipped to the document and labeled Holographic Will.

Last Will and Testament
of
Randall Jones

BE IT KNOWN, that I, Randall Jones, of West Clarke County, in the State of Virginia, being of sound mind, do make, publish, and declare this to be my Last Will and Testament, hereby revoking all my prior Wills and Codicils at any time made.

FIRST: I direct my Personal Representative, herein named

Tera Hensley-Jones, to pay all my just debts and funeral expenses, as soon as may be convenient.

SECOND: All the rest, residue, and remainder of my estate, whether real, personal, or mixed property, I give and bequeath to Tera Hensley-Jones, in total and without exception.

THIRD: In the event that Tera Hensley-Jones shall die with me, predecease me, or not live beyond forty-eight hours after my death, I then give and bequeath my entire estate to Jane Collins and Lauren Jones, the estate to be split evenly between them.

The will was signed at the bottom by Randall. Joe was surprised it wasn't notarized. *Jane and Lauren must be Randall's daughters. I wonder if they know all his money's goin' to Tera? Not anymore.* Joe shut the drawer and walked over to the shredder behind the desk, setting the document inside the slot. The machine grabbed the will and shredded it into tiny pieces.

Joe sat at the desk and opened the laptop. While the computer loaded, he thought, *What does Tera love the most? Definitely not Randall.* Joe thought about Colleen's description of Tera's behavior over the years. The icons appeared on the screen. Her screen-saver image was of herself in a gym, deadlifting, every muscle in her body bulging, a muscled crowd of gym rats cheering in the background. Many of the gym rats, including Tera, wore shirts that read CrossFit Clarke.

Joe inserted the flash drive into the USB port on the side of the laptop. He clicked the icon for the File Explorer and found the flash drive. It held video of Randall, pale and thin, sitting behind the very same desk, where Joe sat at that moment. Randall read the will with a clear but monotone voice. His eyes occasionally drifted off camera, as if seeking approval.

At the end he added, "I love Jane and Lauren, but I do not think they are responsible with money, and I do not want my wealth to be squandered. I trust that Tera will use my wealth wisely. I am of sound mind and body, and these are my wishes." Then, he signed the will, and the video ended.

That's shady. Joe pocketed the flash drive, shoving it in the discreet zipper pocket next to one of his front pockets, and zipping it shut for safekeeping. He wasn't sure yet what he might do with the flash drive, but he had a feeling it was important. Joe clicked on Tera's videos and checked for the holographic will video on her laptop. Joe figured if it was important, the flash drive wasn't the only copy. He found the video, deleted it; then he emptied the virtual trash can, sending the video into the oblivion.

Afterward, Joe clicked on her documents and browsed through Word document titles and folders. Many folders bore the title of someone's name. Joe recognized some of the names as his neighbors, as well as teachers and school employees. Joe thought about what Colleen had said about Tera having dirt on everyone. He clicked the folder labeled Elliot Pratt. Inside were several pictures of Elliot at a bar, kissing a young brunette. Joe clicked on the Word document that was inside the folder titled Elliot Pratt Notes.

-Elliot Pratt is having an affair with his administrative assistant. How cliché! (See pictures.)
-I sent the images from my fake email account to judge his interest. He claims that Linda already knows.
-Elliot threatened to ruin me and asked who I was. I'm soooo scared. Haha!
-I now believe that he is right. Linda doesn't care because

she's having an affair with Colleen. So scandalous!

-I will have to find another way. I think he and Fred may be doing something illegal with the county zoning. The rumor is that Elliot's business is always approved quickly for permits, and other companies are not. I need to poke around and see what I can find.

Joe closed the Word document. Then, he searched for a folder labeled Colleen Wolfe or Wolfe Colleen, but there wasn't one. *Why not? She hated Colleen. She knew Colleen was having an affair with Linda.* Joe checked the list of documents again. He clicked on the folder labeled Dr. Lucas Sellers. Inside was a video and a Word document. The video showed Lucas and Stacy arguing in their backyard, their sparkling blue pool in the background. Lucas smacked Stacy across the face, then stood over her, taunting her, like an NFL linebacker after a big hit. Joe closed the video and opened the Word document titled Dr. Lucas Sellers Notes.

-I sent Lucas the video from my dummy email account, requesting $10,000 in Bitcoin, otherwise I would alert CPS. (I love Bitcoin. Blackmail used to be too risky. Now it's totally anonymous.)

-YES! Just like that, I'm 10K richer. This is too easy.

-I requested another 10K. He initially balked, but he paid on my assurances that it was the final payment.

-I'll wait a few months and ask again. Either he'll pay or I'll turn him in. Either way I win!

Joe closed the Word document and Lucas's folder. Joe scanned the folder names again, finding Fred Nielsen. Joe clicked on the folder, finding several images and a document inside. The pictures showed

Fred at a bar, his arm around another man. One picture showed his hand on the rear end of a man wearing assless chaps. Joe knitted his brow. *Holy shit. Fred's gay?* Joe opened the accompanying document.

> -My PI hit the mother lode! The pictures shocked even me. I can't believe the old stick-up-his-ass is gay!
> -I sent Fred my standard request for $10,000 in Bitcoin. He didn't know how to set up a Bitcoin account, so I told him that Google was his friend. Haha!
> -SUCCESS! I received the payment. We'll see how many payments I can milk out of the old bastard before he taps out.

Joe closed Fred's folder, clicked on Tera's videos, and browsed the thumbnails. Most of the videos were workout instructional videos or apparent blackmail videos. Lucas's abuse video was there. One video was labeled Paul Ambrose Steals from Teacher's Room. Joe knew the name. Paul was a history teacher at the middle school. *Tera has dirt on everyone.*

The workout instructional videos featured the same muscled man. Joe leaned into the screen, squinting. *That's Brock Vickers. He's the gym teacher that Colleen had heard was havin' an affair with Tera.* Joe played a video titled How to Do Kettlebell Swings. Brock stood on the rubber flooring, bare-chested, a kettlebell at his feet. Brock appeared to be in his late-twenties and resembled a blond superhero. A banner hung behind him that read CrossFit Clarke. He explained the exercise; then he demonstrated—widening his stance, swinging the kettlebell between his legs, over his head and back down again, keeping his elbows straight. At the very end of the video Tera said, "That was great."

Tera must've been behind the camera phone.

Joe went back to the video thumbnails. One was labeled Patti

Underwood Cries in My Office. Joe remembered Colleen talking about Patti. She was a teacher at the middle school, although Joe couldn't remember the subject she taught. Joe clicked on the video and watched Patti on a hidden camera, sitting in Tera's office.

"Please reconsider. My husband's divorcing me. I've had some health complications." Patti wiped her eyes, her mascara running. "Please don't do this."

The camera didn't show Tera, but it picked up her audio. Her voice was ice-cold. "I'm not *doing* anything. You did this to yourself. You'll be placed on a teacher improvement plan. If you fail to meet the criteria, I'll have to let you go."

Joe stopped the video. *Why does Tera have this?* Then, it hit him like a bolt of lightning. *To relive the moment over and over again, like a serial killer with a trophy. Power. That's what she loves the most. She loves having power over people. How do I destroy that?* Joe stroked his beard, thinking for several seconds. Then, he smiled to himself. *Humiliate her. Get her fired.*

He went back to the thumbnails, searching for anything humiliating. He found several thumbnails that showed a similar perspective from behind Tera's desk. One was labeled, Teacher Barks Like a Dog. Another was labeled Cougar Time. Joe clicked Teacher Barks Like a Dog, playing the video.

Tera reprimanded a young male teacher for viewing pornography on his school laptop. The teacher begged her for another chance, arguing that he was at home when he viewed the pornography. To save his job, Tera made him crawl around the floor on all fours, barking like a dog. *This could get her fired, but it's not a slam dunk.* Joe went back to the other video, Cougar Time.

In the video, Brock Vickers sat in front of Tera's desk, the same spot where Patti had cried. He wore a sweatsuit with a whistle around his neck. Again, the camera didn't show Tera, but it picked up her audio.

The camera must be in front of Tera.

"You've been a bad boy, Brock," Tera said. "We've had reports of you touching yourself in math class. What do you have to say for yourself?"

Brock dipped his head, chastened. "I'm sorry, Principal Hensley. It's just … my math teacher's really hot. I can't help it."

"Do you think I'm hot?"

Brock lifted his head and grinned. "The hottest."

"That's inappropriate behavior, Brock."

He frowned. "Sorry."

Tera walked from behind the camera to Brock, sitting in front of the desk. She wore heels and a skirt suit. Her gray hair and Brock's youth almost made the role play believable. "It looks like I'll have to call your parents."

Brock swallowed hard. "Please don't, Principal Hensley. My dad will kick my ass."

Tera glared at Brock.

"Butt. Sorry."

Tera sighed. "Well, maybe I can think of something you can do to make it up to me."

"Anything."

Tera hiked up her skirt, revealing muscular thighs and a lack of underwear.

Brock gaped at her crotch. "Principal Hensley? What are you doing?"

Joe raised one side of his mouth in disgust.

Tera kicked off her heels and sat on the edge of her desk in front of Brock.

Joe fast-forwarded the video, catching bits and pieces—Brock performing oral sex, while Tera sat on her desk. Then, Brock bending her over the desk, and Tera wincing for the camera with each thrust.

Joe closed the video and clicked on the Google icon on the bottom taskbar. He smiled as Tera's Gmail opened automatically. Joe composed an email.

From: TeraHensley1122@gmail.com
To:
Subject: My Resignation

Everyone,

I wanted you all to be the first to know that I'm in love. I know that it's inappropriate to engage in a sexual relationship with an employee, but I can't help it. I'm deeply in love.

This is my official resignation as principal of Thomas Jefferson Middle School, West Clarke County, Virginia.

I hope all the West Clarke County school board members eat donkey dicks and die!

Fuck you very much,
Tera Hensley-Jones

Joe attached the Cougar Time video. Then, he searched Tera's contact list, adding anyone who had an email address from the West Clarke County School District—over sixty emails in total. Joe hovered the cursor over the Send button and clicked. "Boom." Joe cackled to himself, as he stood from the desk.

Chapter 32: Kept Man

Joe left Tera's home office and walked past the door to the basement. A faint voice coming from the basement stopped him in his tracks. *Is that Randall?* Joe put his ear to the basement door, but he didn't hear the voice again. Joe opened the door and poked his head down the basement steps. The sunlight from upstairs filtered down the steps, revealing another door at the bottom of the steps. He squinted at the door. *Is that a dead bolt? It looks like an exterior door.* Joe descended the carpeted basement steps, listening as he went. He stopped at the bottom of the stairs. A fiberglass exterior door was locked with a dead bolt.

The hair on the back of Joe's neck stood on end. *Whatever's behind this door, Tera doesn't want it to get out.* Joe put his ear to the door, listening for clues as to what or who might be on the other side. He didn't hear anything, so he unlocked the dead bolt. After the *click* of the dead bolt, he listened again but heard nothing. So, he opened the door and pushed inside. Joe stepped into a hallway. It was dimly lit from the ambient light coming from the room to his right. Joe removed his handgun from his holster. He went left first. At the end of the short hall was a bathroom and bedroom. A hospital bed was inside the dark bedroom. The room smelled like urine. Joe turned around and tiptoed down the hall toward the light.

The voice came again. It was faint. "Safe. Safe. Safe."

Is that Randall?

Joe peered around the corner at the end of the hall. Randall sat on the sectional couch, wearing his pajamas, gaping at a soundless television. Joe thought about running, but he wondered if Randall was a prisoner. He thought about the dead bolt and the will. Joe holstered his weapon. Then, he reached for the light switch at the corner of the wall and turned on the overhead light.

Randall cowered, like a vampire.

Joe approached the couch, with a smile. "Hey, Randall. I was just comin' over to check on you."

Randall squinted up at Joe. His skin was pale, almost translucent, and pulled tight around his skull, giving him a skeletal appearance. He had declined since his appearance on the holographic will video. "Who are you?"

"A friend. Did Tera lock you down here?"

"I don't know who you are."

Randall reminded Joe of Colleen's father, when he had dementia. "My name's John. I'm an old friend. Did Tera lock you down here?"

Randall shook his head. "Tera keeps me safe. She's my angel. Tera keeps me safe. She's my angel." Randall returned his attention to the soundless nature channel.

"The door was locked. Why are you locked down here?"

Randall's eyes glazed over.

Joe moved in front of the wall-mounted flat screen. "Randall. Why are you locked down here?"

"Tera keeps me safe. She's my angel."

Joe spoke slower, enunciating each word. "Did Tera lock you down here?"

"Tera keeps me safe. She's my angel."

Do I call the police? He thought about Linda, taped to a chair in her husband's closet. *I'll go to prison for what I did to her. I'll call after I'm gone. If Tera could do this to her husband, maybe she killed Colleen. I should steal that laptop.* "I'm glad you're doin' okay, Randall. I'm gonna get goin'."

"Tera keeps me safe. She's my angel."

Joe left the way he came in, turning off the overhead light as he went.

He walked down the dim hallway toward the basement door. The basement door was still open, as he had left it. Something near the top of the door caught Joe's attention. *Shit.* There was an alarm contact at the top of the door. Footsteps came from above. *Shit.* Joe had left the upstairs door to the basement open too. The footsteps neared. The *click-clack* on the hardwood sounded like heels. *It must be Tera.*

Joe rushed into the dark bedroom. He grabbed his handgun from his holster and crouched by the wall, next to the open doorway.

The footsteps descended the stairs. Presumably, Tera pushed the basement door open wider, the hinges creaking in response. The footsteps entered the basement, sneaking down the hall toward Randall.

Joe emerged from the bedroom, his handgun trained on her back. "Stop right there."

Tera spun on her bare feet and fired a Taser, the metal prongs sticking into Joe's stomach, the fifty-thousand volts dropping him to the carpet.

He fell awkwardly on his side. His handgun fell from his grasp. Every muscle in his body pulsed with electricity. Joe tried to reach for the prongs, but he couldn't move his hands.

Tera sauntered toward him in bare feet, wearing a pant suit, and holding the Taser on full blast. She moved the Taser to her left hand, still sending fifty-thousand volts to Joe's twitching body. Tera reached into her pocket with her right hand, retrieving a blackjack. With a flick of her wrist the metal baton extended to its full length of eighteen inches. Then, she stopped the electric current. Joe lay on the carpet, spent from the ordeal. Tera reared back with the baton and hit Joe on the temple.

Everything went black.

Chapter 33: Inferno

Joe's eyes fluttered and opened. His vision was blurry, but he couldn't miss the flames surrounding him. Joe coughed and hacked, smoke burning his lungs. The heat covered him, like an electric blanket. His head pounded. He sat on the subflooring of a partially built town house. The wooden bones of the house were ablaze and crackling.

Incoming sirens pierced the air. Joe tried to crawl away, but his left hand was attached to a vertical two-by-four at the end of a skeletal wall. A handcuff was tight around his wrist, connected to a chain, with the chain wrapped around the two-by-four. Joe staggered to his feet, still coughing. He nearly collapsed from the exertion, holding on to the wall assembly for support.

He tapped his hips, checking for his knife and gun, but they were gone. The flames spun around him, his mind fuzzy. *Tera must've drugged me.* When he could stand on his own, Joe gripped the chain with both hands. He frantically yanked backward several times with all his weight, but the two-by-four held.

Sirens blared. Red, white, and blue lights whirred overhead, mixing with the fire, brightening the night sky. Faint voices came from the front of the construction site. From Joe's point of view, he figured he was dead center of the inferno. Joe raised his fleece over his mouth and nose.

His heart pounded. His face and hair dripped with sweat. He

stepped back, the chain now taut. He lowered his stance like a bull, took two quick steps, and jammed his shoulder into the two-by-four. A crack came from the wood, but it held. Joe staggered back and took another run at the two-by-four, smashing through, and falling to the subfloor.

Joe removed the chain from the broken two-by-four. He was free from the wall assembly, but the handcuff was still tight around his left wrist, connected to the second cuff, and that cuff was still attached to the chain. Fire raged around him, smoke billowing into the air. He picked up the heavy chain and spun around, searching for an exit.

No route was clear, but, in the front of the house was a large opening, where the bay window would've been. The wooden frame surrounding the future window was on fire, like the rest of the wood. He took a breath, with his fleece over his mouth and nose. Then, he sprinted for the opening, his boots barely touching the fiery subfloor. Heat came from his back, his fleece catching fire. Like a lion in a carnival stunt, he dove through the fiery window frame, falling four feet to the clay soil. Joe landed on his shoulder, immediately rolling away from the house and extinguishing the flames on his back.

He crawled to the gravel road, hacked, spat, and collapsed. The voices and sirens grew louder. Firefighters sprayed water on the nearby blazing homes. Soon they'd be on the same gravel road as Joe. *I could go to the police, tell them about Tera and Randall.* Joe shook his head. *They won't believe me. Not after what I've done. They'll pin this fire on me too.* He struggled to his feet and staggered toward the woods, his lungs burning, and his world still spinning.

Joe crashed through the brambles into the woods, collapsing in a heap on the leaves. He sucked in the cool night air for several minutes. His hands and wrists were red with minor burns, but the rest of his body was unburned. Firefighters now doused the house he'd just come from with water.

After catching his breath and recovering some of his faculties, Joe rose to his feet and checked his pockets. His pockets were empty, except for Tera's tiny flash drive, which was still in his discreet zipper pocket. Joe found the game trail, with help from the moon, and hiked back toward his stone cabin.

The hike took twice as long as normal. His legs were rubbery, and his mind was fuzzy. His left arm was tired from dragging the handcuffs and chain. His tired shuffle was zombielike. When he finally made it to the creek, he plunged his red hands and wrists into the cold water, feeling immediate relief. Then, he knelt at the water's edge, cupped the water with his hands and drank. Joe unzipped his discreet pocket and removed Tera's flash drive. *She's gonna have a helluva legal fight without this video.* Joe smashed the flash drive with his boot and tossed the remnants in the water.

Joe hiked along the creek back to the stone cabin. The sun rose, providing dim light in the early morning hours. The meows started before he opened the door. Joe entered the cabin, shutting the door behind him. Baby Kitty rushed toward him, meowing.

"I'm okay," Joe said.

BK rose on her hind legs, placing her front paws just above Joe's knees. She said, "*Woo.*"

"I know. I'm sorry for leavin' you for so long. You must be hungry." Joe went to the plastic crates along the wall, while BK was underfoot, incessantly meowing. "I'm gettin' there. Hold on." Joe wrapped the chain around his left arm so it didn't dangle. Then, he put a scoop of dry food in her bowl, and the meowing stopped.

Joe grabbed a hack saw from his tools. He set his left arm, the handcuffs, and the chain on the table. He sawed through the small chain that connected the two handcuffs. This left him with one handcuff that was still around his wrist, but he no longer had the weight of the other cuff or the large chain.

After mostly freeing himself from his chains, Joe undressed and cleaned himself, using a Rubbermaid wash bin, a rag, and soap. He used creek water to wet the rag and stood in the bin to catch the excess water and soap. Joe shivered as he put on clean sweats. Then, he climbed under the covers. BK jumped in bed with Joe, licking the tip of his nose, then lying next to him in a circle.

"We're in trouble, BK," Joe said. "Sooner or later they're gonna find us. We gotta be ready to move when that happens.

BK yawned.

"Okay. We'll talk about it after we rest. I have a lot to tell you." Joe closed his eyes and fell into a deep slumber.

Chapter 34: Double Back

Two days later, dim sunlight filtered through the windows of Joe's stone cabin. Joe sat at the card table, an empty plate and a beef jerky wrapper before him. "I wonder why Tera didn't just shoot me with my own gun. She could've claimed self-defense. I broke into her house."

BK sat on the table, munching on dried cat food.

"Maybe she didn't want the cops to see Randall. Maybe she wanted to get revenge on the Pratts' by burnin' down the town houses. Remember. Tera tried to blackmail Elliot for havin' an affair, but he didn't bite. Then, if I'm burned up in the fire, the cops would find my body and figure I committed the arson and committed suicide in the process. She gets rid of me and has her revenge. What do you think?"

BK finished her food, looked at her empty bowl, and meowed.

"I gave you plenty of food," Joe said.

She meowed again.

"I need you to focus. Tera's the key to everything. She had to be the one who killed Colleen."

BK licked her lips.

"I wonder if she knows I'm alive. Nobody was at the construction site, so I'm assumin' the news would report no casualties."

BK walked across the table and licked the beef jerky wrapper.

Joe sighed. "I don't know what happens after this. I think we're runnin' out of time." Joe petted BK from her head to her tail. "You're not gonna like this, but I need to find a home for you." Joe swallowed the lump in his throat. "If I would've died in that fire, nobody would've been here to feed you. You could've died too. I won't let that happen again."

BK tilted her ears and stood at attention.

Joe listened too.

Faint barking came from outside.

"*Shit.*" Joe rose from his seat and rushed to the door. BK followed. Joe put the cat inside the cat carrier and removed a compass from one of the pockets on the backpack. Then, he put the pack on his back and grabbed his shotgun leaning against the wall. He slung the shotgun across his chest, freeing his hands.

Outside, the barking was noticeably louder and approaching from the south, likely following Joe's tracks along the game trail. Joe ran the short distance toward the creek, the barking perilously close, and coupled with male voices. His breath condensed in the cool air. Red, orange, and yellow leaves hung overhead, and brown ones crunched under his feet.

He ran across the shallow creek, stepping on the large rocks to stay dry. He'd been hunting long enough to know that going through the water wouldn't confuse the bloodhounds, but he wasn't trying to confuse them. He was trying to outrun the handler, a man Joe knew wasn't in the best of shape.

On the other side of the creek, Joe glanced at his watch—*4:17 p.m.* The game trail ran north from Wilshire Commons, and the creek ran west a short distance to the stone cabin. Joe held up his compass, picked a landmark, and ran north through the forest, away from the dogs and the men. When he arrived at the landmark, he plotted another landmark, as far north as he could see, and ran to that one. He did this several times. As the voices and barks faded away, Joe checked his watch—*4:22 p.m.*

Joe turned, using his compass to set his route east, hopefully parallel to the creek and perpendicular to the trail. He was hoping to catch the game trail and double back. A few minutes later, he found the narrow game trail. Then, he ran south on the trail, back toward the creek. Joe glanced at his watch again, figuring he'd have to run another five minutes or so on the game trail to make it back to the creek. By then, hopefully the bloodhounds and cops would be following his big circular route through the woods.

Five minutes later he slowed to a walk, his breathing heavy, and the trickle of water nearby. He crept toward the creek, listening for men and dogs. As his breath regulated, he heard faint barking behind him. *Perfect. They're right where I want 'em.* Joe jogged on the game trail at a steady pace, making it to Wilshire Commons in a half hour.

Joe stopped at the edge of the Virginia state game lands, looking at Wilshire Commons. The setting sun cast the arson crime scene in an orange glow. Many of the townhomes had been reduced to piles of ash. Others still stood but were charred black. A police cruiser blocked the entrance to the community, pointing toward Big Oak Lane.

Baby Kitty meowed in the backpack cat carrier.

Joe turned his head and spoke over his shoulder. "I know that was bumpy. I'm sorry for all the runnin'."

Joe hiked around Wilshire Commons, using the forest as concealment. He arrived at the corner of the state game lands, which was a stone's throw from the Sellers's backyard. It was nearly dark, the last bit of sun fading fast. Next door was Tera's house—his ultimate destination. The Sellers's house appeared deserted. So did Tera's. *She has to be home. She wouldn't move Randall. Someone might find out what she's doin' to him.*

Baby Kitty meowed again.

"I know. You're right. She has a Taser, and she's probably ready for us." Joe stroked his beard. "I bet she's not ready for somethin' as simple as the doorbell."

BK said, "*Woo.*"

"Trust me." Joe ran from the woods to Tera's privacy fence. He set the shotgun on the ground, along with BK and the backpack to mostly conceal the firearm. "I'll be right back."

Joe crept around the side of the house to the front corner of the garage. He peered out from the corner, spotting two more police cruisers on Wilshire Lane. The nearest cruiser was directly in front of Fred's house, next door to Tera. The other was parked in front of the Pratts' mansion. *I bet Tera never told anyone I was at her house.*

He snuck around the garage, crouching and walking behind the thick hedges along the house. He stopped at the corner of the stoop, hidden by an eight-foot-tall blue juniper, shaped like a rocket ship. Joe stood behind the juniper and reached out—only his arm revealed for a split second—and pressed the doorbell.

Joe rushed back the way he came, trying to run while bent over beneath the five-foot-tall boxwood hedges. Once he made it to the garage, he sprinted to the back gate. He hopped the fence and opened the locked gate. Joe strapped his shotgun to his chest and grabbed BK in the cat carrier. He shut the gate behind them and hurried to the window he'd broken two days prior. It was covered in clear plastic, awaiting repair. Joe poked a hole with his shotgun barrel. Then, he ripped it open with his hand and slipped inside.

Joe stepped into the family room and set the backpack cat carrier on the sectional couch. He grabbed a thick cushion, his shotgun still strapped to his chest. Between the kitchen and the family room was a short hallway that led to the front door and the stairwell. The front door slammed shut. Joe tiptoed to the corner of the wall, next to the hallway, still holding the large couch cushion. Footsteps came from the hallway. He stood with his back flat against the wall, waiting for Tera.

Baby Kitty meowed.

Shit.

The footsteps stopped, and a sharp inhale of breath came from the hallway. Joe sprang from his hiding spot and rushed Tera, holding the couch cushion out front, like a shield, hoping like hell she wasn't holding his gun. Tera shot her Taser, striking the couch cushion. Joe tossed the cushion aside and smashed the butt of his shotgun across her face, dropping her, like a sack of potatoes.

Chapter 35: Reality

Joe stood over Tera in the hallway, pointing his shotgun at her. "Hurts, doesn't it?"

Tera groaned. "Why are you doing this to me?"

"I know what you did."

"I didn't do anything. I barely know you."

"Stand up," Joe said, still pointing his shotgun at her.

Tera rose to her feet, her legs wobbly. Blood leaked from a cut on her cheek. A red welt already grew in the same place. "Why are you breaking into my house again?"

Joe glared at Tera. "You're gonna do exactly as I say, or I'll blow your fuckin' head off. Got me?"

Tera nodded, her dark eyes glassy.

"Gimme your phone."

Tera reached into the side pocket of her yoga pants, extracting her phone, and handing it to Joe.

Joe snatched her phone and put it into his back pocket. "Hands up."

Tera raised her hands over her head.

"This way." Joe prodded her into the family room. He circled around her, keeping his shotgun pointed at her head. Then, he grabbed the cat carrier, strapping it to one shoulder. Joe motioned with his shotgun back to the hallway. "Let's go. We're goin' upstairs."

Tera walked down the hallway and up the spiral staircase, with Joe right behind her, pointing his rifle at her back.

They went to Tera's master bedroom at the end of the hallway. Joe closed the door behind them and locked it. The blinds and curtains were shut, and the lights were on. A king-size canopy bed dominated the room, with matching bedside tables. Joe prodded her beyond the bed, past the sitting area with a short bookcase and a couch, and ultimately to the bathroom. The bathroom was larger than Joe's stone cabin, with a jacuzzi tube, shower with multiple showerheads, water closet, and his and hers sinks.

"Lay on the floor," Joe said.

Tera turned to Joe, her brow furrowed.

Joe motioned with his shotgun. "On the fuckin' floor. Face-first."

Tera lay face-first on the tile floor.

"Put your hands on the back of your head and don't move."

Tera complied.

Joe went to the sink and grabbed a glass from the countertop. Every second or so, he glanced at Tera, making sure she was still. He filled it to the brim with water and sat it on the floor. Then, he removed the cat carrier backpack from his shoulder. He unzipped the cat carrier and Baby Kitty hopped out. Joe opened the side pocket and removed a plastic sandwich bag filled with dried cat food. BK meowed, her eyes following the food. Joe dumped the cat food on the tile next to the water. BK crunched her food, purring as she ate.

Tera raised her head, gawking at BK. "What the hell is this?"

Joe pointed his shotgun at her face. "Shut up."

Barking came from outside.

"*Shit.*" Joe rushed to the rear window near the jacuzzi tub and split the blinds. The bloodhounds and a team of police officers crept from the state game lands toward Tera's privacy fence, their guns drawn.

Joe grabbed Tera's cell phone from his back pocket and tapped 9-1-1, alternating his gaze from Tera to the cops outside and back again.

"Nine-one-one, what is your emergency?" the operator asked.

"This is Joe Wolfe. I'm holding Tera Jones hostage at her house on Wilshire Lane in Clarke. Police officers are outside this house. If they come in, I will kill her. I suggest you tell them to back off." Joe disconnected the call.

He hustled back to Tera. "Get up."

Tera stood.

Joe pushed her to the window. "Open the blinds and the window."

Tera pulled the string, raising the blinds. Her eyes widened at the police entering her backyard.

Joe pressed the barrel of his shotgun into the back of her neck. "Hurry up."

She unlocked the window and opened it, a cold breeze filtering inside.

"Tell them to back off, or I'll kill you."

"Please get back, or he'll kill me," Tera said through the open window.

A few cops looked up, but many didn't hear.

Joe jabbed her in the head with the barrel of his gun. "Louder!"

Tera winced and shouted, "Get back, or he'll kill me!"

Joe poked his shotgun barrel out the window.

One of the cops shouted, "Gun!"

The cops retreated back to the privacy fence, taking cover outside the fence.

"Shut the window," Joe said.

Tera shut the window.

Joe prodded her from the bathroom, shutting BK inside, not wanting Tera to grab her. Joe pushed the barrel of his shotgun into Tera's back, pushing her to the sitting area. "Let's go. Sit on the couch."

Tera sat on the couch and wiped the corners of her eyes. "What will you do to me?"

"Nothin' if you tell me the truth about what you did to Colleen," Joe said, holding the shotgun comfortably at his hip, using the shoulder strap to hold the weight, but still pointing the weapon at Tera.

She shook her head. "I have no idea what you're talking about."

"You killed her. I know it was you."

"This is crazy. Colleen and I had our differences, but I would never hurt her. I would never hurt anyone."

Joe stepped closer to Tera, glaring, his shotgun pointed in her face. "Really? You didn't chain me up and try to burn me alive?"

Tera knitted her brow. "What?"

"You know exactly what you did."

She drew back, her hand to her chest. "You think I tried to burn you alive?"

Joe stared, his face like stone.

"I'm assuming you're talking about the fire the other night?"

"I bet you thought I was gonna die in that fire. You'd be rid of me, and you'd get back at the Pratts' for not invitin' you to their parties. The police would assume I committed the arson, so you'd be free and clear."

Tera ran her hand over her face. "Do you hear yourself? This is totally insane. You think I started that fire because I was upset about not going to their stupid parties?"

Joe opened his mouth to reply, but nothing came out.

"I was never uninvited. Randall and I stopped going when he got sick. I certainly didn't start that fire. Look. I'm not trying to be combative, especially with a gun in my face, but I think you're having a psychotic break. I was a school psychologist before I became a principal. I've seen it before."

The vein in Joe's neck bulged. "Shut the fuck up."

Tera showed her palms. "I'm trying to help you, Joe. People who go through traumatic events, like losing a spouse, can lose their grip on reality. Are you sure you didn't start that fire?"

"No. Shut up. You knocked me out and drugged me. I woke up in a fuckin' inferno."

Tera dropped her hands to her lap. "You don't remember what happened, do you?"

"I remember."

"You broke into my home and I shot you with my Taser."

Joe nodded. "That's true."

"You fell awkwardly, and you hit your head on the corner of the wall. You were knocked out for a minute, maybe less. I took your gun and called the police, but you woke up and ran away before the police came."

"That's not what happened. You chained me to a burning house. I almost died."

Tera held out her hands. "How would I do that, Joe? You think I could drag you up the stairs and across the construction site? I might work out, but I'm still an old lady."

Joe let go of his shotgun, the shoulder strap holding it to his body. He shook his head, pacing back and forth in front of Tera on the couch. "No. That can't be right. No. No. No." He hit himself several times on the head with his open palm.

"I don't know if you started the fire that night or not, but I certainly didn't."

Sirens sounded in the distance.

Joe rushed to the window in the sitting area, splitting the blinds. Police cars raced to the scene, parking on Wilshire Lane in front of Tera's house. Joe turned back to Tera.

She was on the edge of her seat, ready to run.

"Don't even think about it."

Tera flashed her palms and sat back. "I wasn't thinking anything."

Joe went back to pacing in front of the couch. "Shit. Shit. Shit."

"If you turn yourself in, I'll tell them that you didn't hurt me," Tera said.

Joe pivoted and trained his shotgun on Tera again. "You're a liar. I know what you're doin' to Randall, keepin' him caged, like an animal."

Tera shook her head. "I keep my husband locked in the basement while I'm gone for his own safety. If I didn't, he'd go outside, get lost, and freeze to death. He's not a prisoner. He has dementia."

"You're a *liar*. He's malnourished."

"He's old, and he forgets to eat."

Joe narrowed his eyes, searching Tera's face for signs of deception. "Doesn't mean you didn't kill Colleen. I know all about the dirt you collect for your bribery schemes. You killed Colleen because you couldn't stand it that she had somethin' on you."

"This is crazy, Joe. There are no bribery schemes. I do keep up with the rumor mill but for my protection. Do you know how many teachers have tried to get me fired? Your wife was one of them. Is that why you sent that *very* personal video? For revenge? To ruin my life?"

Tera's cell phone chimed in Joe back pocket. Joe flinched, then grabbed the phone from his pocket. He stared at the phone number.

"You should answer that," Tera said. "It's probably the police."

Chapter 36: The Hostage Negotiator

"Hello," Joe said, the cell phone to his ear.

"This is Detective Bryce Young of the West Clarke County Police Department. Is this Joe Wolfe?"

"Yes."

The detective's voice was calm, yet concerned, without a trace of anger. "How are you doing, Joe? We had a call from you that you're with Tera Jones."

Joe paced in front of Tera, who still sat on the couch. "Yeah."

"Is she okay?"

"She's fine."

"May I speak with her for confirmation?"

"Hold on." Joe turned to Tera. "The detective wants to know if you're okay." Joe held out the phone to Tera.

She reached for the phone.

Joe pulled it back. "Don't touch it. Just talk." He held it near her face again.

"This is Tera Hensley-Jones. I'm okay."

Joe put the phone back to his ear. "See? She's fine."

"What about Randall Jones? Is he in the house with you?" the detective asked.

Joe went back to pacing in the sitting area, and keeping watch on Tera. "I think he's in the basement. I haven't seen him."

"I'd love to send a medical professional inside to check on him—"

"*No.* Nobody comes inside."

"Okay. You're in charge, Joe. Can you tell me how you got into this situation? Maybe I can help."

Joe told the detective why he thought Tera had killed Colleen and about the proof he had uncovered. Detective Young mostly listened and asked a few clarification questions. At one point Joe had addressed the police officer as detective, to which the officer had replied, "Please call me Bryce."

Twenty minutes later, Joe finally stopped talking and stopped pacing. The white carpet in front of the couch was matted from Joe's boots. He stared at Tera, sitting on the couch. When he focused on her wrinkles and oval glasses and gray hair, it was hard to imagine that she was a killer. If not for her muscly CrossFit body, she resembled someone's grandmother.

"I'm really sorry about Colleen," Bryce said.

"*Sorry* won't bring her back," Joe replied.

"Neither will holding Tera hostage."

Joe spoke through gritted teeth. "She needs to be held accountable."

"This is a very difficult situation, and I can understand why you think Tera was involved with Colleen's death, and, if she is, I assure you that we'll do everything in our power to give you and Colleen the justice you both deserve. Having said that, I'm obliged to bring something important to your attention."

"What's that?"

Bryce hesitated for an instant. "You mailed us a suicide note."

Joe knitted his brow. "A suicide note? What are you talkin' about?"

"Would you like me to read it to you?"

"Okay. Yeah."

"West Clarke County PD. I murdered my wife. I didn't mean to, but I got so angry that I couldn't control myself. I snapped. I was out of control. I'm so sorry. I need help, but I don't think there's anyone who can fix me. I wish I could take it back. I wish I could go back in time and change it. I thought I could live with what I did, but I can't. It's time for me to go. You can find my ashes where my home once stood. Joe Wolfe."

Joe stood slack-jawed. "That can't be. I didn't write that. Is there a signature?"

"No signature. It's printed."

"I don't have a printer. I don't even have a computer."

"You were using Tera's computer on the same day the suicide note was postmarked. I'm assuming you sent the resignation email posing as Tera."

Joe removed the phone from his ear, dropping his hand to his side. He closed his eyes, picturing using Tera's computer, and placing the letter in the blue mail bin down the street. He pictured his hands around Colleen's neck. Joe opened his eyes. Tera had moved to the edge of the couch, like she was about to bolt. Joe pointed the shotgun at Tera. "Don't do it. Sit back."

Tera leaned back.

"Joe. Are you still there?" Bryce asked, barely audible through the speaker.

Joe put the phone back to his ear. "I'm here. Somethin's not right. I didn't do it. I know I didn't."

"Didn't do what, Joe?"

Joe let go of his shotgun—the shoulder strap holding it to his body—and hit himself in the head with his open palm. "I didn't send that note. I didn't kill my wife. You have to believe me. Please. You have to believe me."

"I do, Joe. I trust you, but I need you to trust me too."

Joe nodded to himself and said, "Okay."

Tera observed Joe.

"There is one really easy thing we could do right now that would be good for everyone involved," Bryce said.

"What's that?" Joe asked.

"If Tera's abusing her husband, as you say, let us examine him. We'll be able to tell if he's being abused or not. In good faith, let Randall go. He's innocent, and he needs medical care."

Joe stroked his beard for a moment, thinking. "I'll do it, but I want somethin' first."

"What do you want?" Bryce asked.

"I want my daughter to call me. Tell her that she can't hang up on me. She has to hear me out." Joe gave the detective Emily's cell phone number, then he disconnected the call.

Joe sneered at Tera. "When my daughter calls, you're gonna tell her the truth, or I will kill you."

Chapter 37: Emily

"I have to pee," Tera said, sitting on the couch, her knee bouncing up and down.

Joe stood on the carpet, facing her, his shotgun resting against the shoulder sling, and pointed vaguely in her direction. "I don't care. Piss your pants."

Tera frowned.

The cell phone chimed in Joe's back pocket. Joe answered the phone. "Emily. Is it you?"

Her voice was clipped and tight. "It's me. What do you want?"

Joe took a deep breath. "Look. I know you think I killed your mother, but I didn't. I swear to you." Joe paused, waiting for a response that never came. "I don't expect you to believe me, so I found proof. I found the person who did it. She's gonna tell you the truth." Joe glowered at Tera, cementing that point.

"What are you doing, Dad?" Emily replied. "You're only making things worse. You have to let that woman go."

"Not until she tells the truth. I'm puttin' you on Speaker." Joe put the phone on Speaker and held it near Tera. "Go ahead, tell her what you did to Colleen."

Tera pressed her lips together.

Joe pointed his shotgun at her face. "*Tell her.*"

Tera swallowed hard. "I was Colleen's principal. We didn't always get along. I should've been nicer to her." Tera hesitated. "Colleen was very creative and emotional. I used to get angry when she forgot procedural details. I didn't always give her the best evaluations. I was wrong. I shouldn't have done that. She was really great with the kids. I'm sorry. I wish I could still tell her that—"

"Tell her the fuckin' truth!"

Tera flinched.

"Dad, *stop*," Emily said, her voice coming from the speaker.

"Tell her how you killed Colleen," Joe said.

Tera's eyes were wet. "I killed Colleen."

Joe jabbed Tera's chest with the shotgun barrel. "Tell her exactly what happened!"

Tera leaned back, away from the shotgun. "I don't know what happened. Tell me what I'm supposed to say, and I'll say it. I'll say whatever you want."

Joe hit her in the face with the butt of his shotgun.

Tera yelped and slouched on the couch, holding her nose, blood running between her fingers.

"Did you just hit her?" Emily asked.

"She killed her," Joe said.

Tera groaned and lifted her shirt, exposing her sports bra and toned abs. She held her shirt to her nose to catch the blood.

"That's *enough*, Dad," Emily said. "I don't care what she says. I won't believe it."

"She did it. I know she did," Joe said.

"You need professional help. You're not well. The police can help you. Please turn yourself in."

Joe tapped the phone taking it off Speaker. He placed the cell to his ear. "Please, Em. You have to believe me. I'm tellin' the truth."

"If you ever want me to talk to you again, you'll let her go and turn yourself in. Otherwise, I have nothing to say to you."

Joe walked a few paces away from Tera but still kept an eye on her. "Do you remember when you used to come with me in the truck when I made short hauls?"

Emily exhaled. "I remember."

"You used to be my best friend, next to your mother. You always had so many questions about everything. That's when I knew you were so smart. Smarter than me, even when you were little. You remember that?"

Emily sniffled.

"I'm sorry, Em." Joe's voice wavered. "I wish things were different."

"So do I."

His eyes were glassy. "I know I'm in no position to make requests of you, but I have a cat. I raised her since she was a kitten. Her name's Baby Kitty or BK for short. She responds to either name. She's been a good friend to me. I was hopin' you could take her. Otherwise, they'll send her to the shelter. I'm sure Matty would love a pet." Joe was referring to his two-year-old grandson, whom he'd never met. "Will you please do that for me?"

"If you let that woman go and turn yourself in."

Joe blinked, and tears slipped down his cheeks. "I will. Whatever happens to me, I want you to know that I love you." After a long silence, Joe said, "Bye, honey." He disconnected the call.

Chapter 38: The Ultimatum

Joe wiped his face with the sleeves of his fleece. Tera held her head back, stemming the tide of blood. The cell phone chimed.

"Yeah," Joe answered.

"Your daughter loves you," Bryce said. "She wants you to turn yourself in."

Joe blew out a breath. "I think it's too late for that."

"It's not too late. I'll put in a good word with the DA. Everyone can go home safe."

Joe shook his head. "Not me. I don't get to go home." Joe narrowed his eyes at Tera. "She's gonna admit what she did."

Bryce paused for an instant. "I gave you what you asked for, now you need to let Randall go."

"You got any EMTs out there?"

"We have several paramedics and an ambulance."

"Two EMTs can come in and get Randall. He's in the basement. Under no circumstances are they to come upstairs, and I don't want any cops comin' inside either. If they do, I'll blow her brains out. Got me?"

"You're the boss, Joe. I'll have the paramedics come get Randall right away, and they'll stay downstairs. Don't worry. No police officers. I'll call you before they enter the house."

"Okay." Joe disconnected the call, slipped the phone into his back pocket, and walked over to Tera on the couch.

She sat upright, her T-shirt stained with blood, and her nostrils ringed with dried blood. "You should listen to Emily."

Joe curled his lips into a sneer. "Say her name again, and I'll knock your teeth out your mouth."

Tera dipped her head in deference. "This won't end well for you."

"Get up."

Tera stood from the couch.

"Let's go." Joe pushed her toward the door.

They walked out of the master bedroom, Joe following Tera. Red, white, and blue lights whirred through the windows, mixing with the artificial light from the fridge-size chandelier that hung in the foyer. They descended the spiral staircase and walked to the front door.

"Stop," Joe said, halting Tera ten feet from the front door. He walked around her, unlocked the door, and glanced out the sidelight window. The house was surrounded by police cruisers and officers with rifles and spotlights pointed in his direction. Joe retracted his head from the window and returned to Tera. "All right. Back upstairs." Joe marched Tera upstairs to the landing, which held a view of the front door. He forced her to lay on her stomach.

A few minutes later, Bryce called. "Two paramedics are at the door."

"Send 'em in," Joe replied.

The paramedics entered the front door, one carrying a medical kit. Joe eyed them, his shotgun pointed at Tera on the carpet. One of the paramedics glanced up at Joe, then quickly looked away. They found the door to the basement and disappeared from view.

"I still have to pee," Tera said.

"I still don't care. Piss your pants," Joe replied.

Several minutes later, the paramedics appeared, escorting Randall. The old man moved at a snail's pace, wearing a dingy robe and slippers. He spoke softly to himself, the barely audible mantra carrying through the cavernous house. "Tera keeps me safe. She's my angel. Tera keeps me safe. She's my angel. Tera keeps me safe. She's my angel."

Joe looked down at Tera. "You're screwed. They're gonna find out what you did to him."

"I didn't do anything to him. He has dementia," Tera replied, her face on the carpet.

The paramedics and Randall left the house, shutting the front door behind them.

"Get up. Back to your room," Joe said.

Tera rose from the carpet and walked down the hall to her master bedroom, with Joe following close behind.

Tera stopped and turned around at the couch in the sitting area, facing Joe. She shifted from one foot to the other. "I really have to go. I can't hold it anymore."

Joe jabbed the barrel of his shotgun into her chest, forcing her to step back. "Sit the fuck down."

Tera sat on the couch.

Joe glared down at Tera, remembering the smell that came from Colleen's dead body, the lack of dignity that had accompanied her murder. Joe inched closer, his lower jaw jutting forward, his body trembling with rage. "After what you did to Colleen, I think you can sit in your own piss." Joe stepped back. "Go on. Do it."

A dark stain spread across the crotch of Tera's silver yoga pants. Her eyes were glassy. She wiped her eyes with her index finger, lifting her glasses in the process. The smell of ammonia with a hint of rotten fish wafted through the air.

Joe wrinkled his nose. "You stink. After this, you might wanna see a doctor. Your gym teacher probably gave you an STD." Joe chuckled. "Or maybe you gave one to him."

Tera hung her head and slid across the couch, now sitting next to the bookshelf, and leaving a dark stain on the cushion.

The cell phone chimed.

Joe reached into his back pocket, grabbed the phone, and said, "Yeah."

"Thank you for letting Randall go," Bryce said. "It was the right thing to do."

"Do you see what I'm talkin' about? She brainwashed him to get his money."

"We don't know anything yet. He's receiving medical attention."

"When will you know?"

"That's impossible to say for sure, but we will investigate your claims."

Joe grunted. "Are you playin' me?"

"No. I'm being honest."

Joe grunted again.

"How are you and Tera doing in there? Is everyone safe? Do you or Tera need any food or medical care?"

"We're fine."

"Good. That's great. I'd love to talk to her to confirm."

Joe eyed Tera. She sat on the couch, her crotch wet, and her head hanging. "We're not doin' that again. She's fine. You'll have to take my word for it."

"What's next, Joe?"

"I want you to open Colleen's murder case, and I want Tera to be investigated as the prime suspect."

Bryce hesitated for a few seconds. "We can do that, but it would require that you release her into our custody."

Joe shook his head again and paced in front of Tera on the couch, and the chest-high bookcase filled with hardback novels. "If I let her go, you'll kill me."

"If you surrender, I guarantee that we won't hurt you. All you have to do is put down that shotgun and walk out the front door with your hands up. That's it. I promise you, Joe. We won't hurt you."

"You'll lock me up for the rest of my life."

"No. You're not a criminal, Joe. You need help. I can get you into a treatment facility, so you can get the help you need."

"No. No. No." Joe smacked himself on the head with an open palm. "There's nothin' wrong with me."

"Of course. You just need some help."

Joe smacked himself again. "No. No. No. I want a million dollars and a private plane to take me to Panama."

"Joe. Be reasonable," Bryce replied. "We're almost out of this."

"Get me my fuckin' money and my plane, or she dies. You have one hour." Joe disconnected the call. The phone chimed again. Joe answered. "Don't call me until you have my plane and my money. One hour or she dies."

"Joe. Please—"

Joe disconnected the call again and stashed the phone back in his pocket.

Tera raised her gaze, her face tear-streaked. "You're crazy. They won't let you go."

"An hour from now I'll be on a plane, and you'll be under investigation."

Tera rolled her eyes.

Chapter 39: A Clean Conscience

A half hour later, the cell phone chimed.

Joe took a few steps away from Tera and answered the cell phone, now standing in front of the bookcase next to the couch. "You got my plane and my money?"

Bryce replied, "Look, Joe. I'm working very hard to get you what you want, but I need a little more time."

Joe frowned. "How much more time?"

"A few hours."

"What does that mean? Two hours? Three? I need an exact time."

"Three hours. Hopefully."

Joe furrowed his brow. "*Hopefully?*"

"You're asking for a lot, Joe. I can get the plane and the money, but I need some time. Three, maybe four hours. In the meantime, do you need anything? Food? Medical care?"

Joe lowered the volume on the phone, silencing Bryce, not wanting to hear from him anymore. "You have two hours. I'm killing her if I don't have my money and my plane." Joe slammed the phone facedown on the bookcase, within reach of Tera, sitting at the end of the couch.

"They'll kill you if you don't let me go," Tera said.

Joe turned to Tera and shot her a look that could kill. "Shut up. You should worry about yourself. Your life is fucked. I already ruined your career and your reputation."

"I'm not worried. I'll be a hero after this. The school board will make your little email go away. It was sent illegally by an insane psychopath."

Joe stepped in front of Tera, his shotgun dangling from the shoulder strap, and pointed in her direction. "You're wrong. Every student in the county has already downloaded your video. You'll never work in education again. Next stop for you is prison. You think I won't tell the cops about your blackmail scams? You think I won't tell them how you tried to burn me alive?"

Tera leaned back on the couch, a self-satisfied smirk on her face. "*Jesus*, Joe. You really are crazy. You already told the detective about all your so-called proof. He wasn't compelled because it's all bullshit. There's no proof of anything."

"You think I told him everything? I have plenty of evidence against you. Did you know that I've been in your school office too?"

Tera shrugged, that smirk still on her face. "You're lying."

"Louise let me into your office after hours." Joe was referring to the head custodian. "Man, I found a ton of stuff. Louise was pissed about the way you treated Colleen."

Tera sat up straight. Her smirk evaporated.

"You know Colleen and Louise were good friends, right?"

"You're lying."

"There'll be investigations to find the truth. What do you think Fred or Lucas might say about bein' blackmailed?"

Tera pressed her lips together.

Joe raised his eyebrows. "You sure you didn't leave any DNA at the arson? What about your gas can? Will the cops find that you went to the gas station that day and filled the can? What about the handcuffs and chain you used to tie me to that house? I cut 'em off but I still have 'em." Joe stroked his beard. "I wonder if your fingerprints are on 'em?"

Tera clenched her jaw.

"What about your cell phone? They can track you pretty good with that.

Did you have your phone on you, when you set that fire?" Joe grinned. "You know what? Once these investigations get movin', I bet they'll find evidence connectin' you to Colleen's murder. I bet they'll find things that I don't even know about. I bet what I know is just the tip of the iceberg."

"You're delusional."

Joe tilted his head. "Really? You don't sound convinced, but don't worry. I have a solution for you. Once Randall dies, which is probably soon, you can take your inheritance and disappear. He looks rough by the way. You haven't been a very good caregiver."

"Fuck you."

"The way I see it, takin' the money and runnin' is your only way out. Maybe we can hang out in Panama. What do you think?"

She glared up at Joe.

Joe snapped his fingers. "Shit, that won't work. I forgot. I shredded Randall's will and destroyed that flash drive. I made sure to erase the video from your laptop too. You might be thinkin' I'm a dumbass, and you'll just fish it out of the Recycle Bin, but I deleted it there too."

Tera clenched her fists, her forearm muscles flexing in response.

"You might be able to get Randall to sign another will, but good luck gettin' him to read it again for the camera, him not being of sound mind. I bet it'll be hard to prove the validity of the will without that video." Joe chuckled. "Seems like you're just as screwed as me."

Tera took a deep breath, unclenched her fists, and smiled. "I doubt that. You're living in a complete fantasy. They'll never give you a million dollars and a plane trip. They're just buying time. Eventually, they'll storm this house, and they'll kill you."

Joe pointed his shotgun at her face. "*Shut up.*"

One side of her mouth raised in contempt. "You're leaving here in handcuffs or a body bag. Those are your only options."

"Shut the *fuck* up."

Tera rolled her eyes but sat quietly.

Joe paced back and forth, his shotgun dangling from his shoulder strap, and Tera's warnings worming their way into his psyche. After several minutes, Joe stopped pacing and faced Tera. "You don't know what you're talkin' about."

Tera shrugged. "Maybe. I doubt you would bring it up again if you thought I was wrong."

Joe pointed at her for emphasis. "I'm gonna get my money and my flight, and the cops are gonna arrest you for murderin' Colleen."

"You're forgetting something very important."

"What?"

"The truth. Colleen told me about how you abused her—"

"*Shut up.*"

"You almost killed her when you assaulted her. She was afraid of you, and she had good reason."

Joe shook his head, as if he were trying to expel the memory by force. "No. No. No. It's not true."

"She told me that she finally felt safe when you were in prison. Then you came home and killed her."

Joe smacked his forehead with his open palm over and over again. "Shut up. Shut up. Shut up."

"You're the one who knows all about evidence, don't you?"

"No. No. No. Shut up. Shut up."

"Your DNA was found on the gloves that strangled your wife. *You* killed her. That's why your daughter hates you."

Joe dropped to his knees and covered his ears. "Stop it. Stop it. Stop it. It's not true."

Tera scooted to the edge of the couch, her eyes on Joe's shotgun, dangling from the shoulder harness. "You have a mental problem, Joe. You need help. You're not in touch with reality. *You* broke into my house and held me at gunpoint. *You* tried to kill yourself in the fire. *You* killed Colleen."

Joe imagined himself strangling Colleen. Tears welled in his eyes. He thought of Emily and her hatred for him. Joe slumped back on his haunches, hung his head, and sobbed.

Tera stood and grabbed the shoulder harness, easily taking the shotgun from Joe. She pointed the shotgun at Joe, her finger on the trigger. "You're a pathetic piece of shit."

Joe looked up with tears in his eyes and said, "I'm not afraid of you. You're nothin'."

"The last person who underestimated me was Colleen."

"You're wrong. She *beat* you."

Tera smirked at Joe. "Colleen didn't know who she was fucking with." She pursed her lips, her dark eyes alive. "She went down so easy. One hit with the baton. Less than five minutes to strangle that bitch."

Joe sat up straight, his eyes wide. "My gloves from the trash can?"

Tera cackled, looking down on Joe from behind the shotgun barrel. "They fit right over mine. Now stand up."

Joe stood in front of Tera, the shotgun pointed at his chest.

Tera narrowed her eyes, aiming. She raised one side of her mouth in contempt. Then, she pulled the trigger. *Click.* Tera checked the shotgun in disbelief. She quickly racked the pump action. *Chick-chuck.* She pulled the trigger again. *Click.*

Joe smiled and shrugged.

She threw the shotgun at Joe and ran for the door.

He caught the shotgun, turned, and watched her run from the master bedroom. Then, he set the unloaded gun on the couch and went to the window. Tera ran out of the house, into the spotlight. Five police officers approached her, their rifles drawn.

She turned and pointed at the house. Even through the window glass and the commotion, Joe heard Tera say, "He's still inside."

"Put your hands up," one of the officers said.

Tera raised her hands. "He's still inside."

"On your stomach," the officer said.

She hesitated.

"On your stomach! *Now*," the officer shouted.

Tera lay in her front yard, face-first. A police officer wrenched her hands behind her back and handcuffed them.

"What are you doing?" she shrieked. "He's inside."

Joe walked over to the bookcase next to the couch and picked up Tera's cell phone. He turned up the volume so he could hear the detective. "You still there, Bryce?"

"I'm here. Are you okay?"

Joe sat on the armrest of the couch. "I'm fine. Did you get all that?"

"Yeah. We got it. You're lucky. We almost sent in a team."

Joe let out a tired breath. "I don't know if I'd call myself lucky."

Bryce paused for an instant. "I don't know if this'll end the way you want it to."

"I know that."

"You need to come out now."

"I know that too." Joe stood from the couch. "I have a favor to ask."

"As long as it's not a million dollars or a trip to Panama, I'll see what I can do."

"Sorry about that. I wanted her to think I was crazy, and I wanted you guys to give us some time together."

"You had me going. You just ruined your insanity defense though."

Joe laughed, but the detective wasn't laughing with him.

"What's the request?" Bryce asked, cutting through the laughter.

Joe cleared his throat. "My cat's up here in the bathroom. I want you to take her to my daughter's house. She lives about half-an-hour from here—"

"I know where she lives. I can do that. Is that it?"

"Can I have a few minutes to say goodbye?"

"Don't disconnect this call. Let me know when you're coming out."

"Thanks, Bryce." Joe set the phone on top of the bookcase and walked to the bathroom. Joe opened the door.

Baby Kitty meowed and ran to Joe.

He bent down and picked her up, carrying her to the jacuzzi tub. "It's over. Tera admitted to killin' Colleen." Joe sat on the side of the tub, the tile edge providing plenty of room to sit. He set BK in his lap. She kneaded his thigh, then flopped in his lap.

"I know. I'm shocked she admitted it too." Joe petted the cat. "It's an empty feelin' though. It's like I was keepin' Colleen alive with all this. Now there's nothin' left. I know you understand."

BK stretched out her paws, reaching while on her side, then retracting her limbs into a tight circle.

"Don't get too comfortable." Joe swallowed the lump in his throat, still petting the cat. "I'm gonna have to leave soon, and I'm not sure if I'll see you again."

BK purred.

"I don't want you to worry. Emily's gonna take good care of you. She's like Colleen. Loves animals. I know she'll love you too. You'll have a nice house, far better than what you're used to." Joe took a deep breath. "I think I'd be dead if I didn't find you that night in the asparagus patch. You gave me ... purpose. You're my best friend, BK." Joe bent over and kissed the cat on the top of her head.

BK gazed up at Joe with those big round eyes.

"I have to go now." Joe picked up BK and set her on the floor.

She followed Joe as he walked toward the door.

Joe shut her in the bathroom.

BK meowed over and over again.

"I'm sorry, BK," he said through the bathroom door. Then, he walked to the bookcase and picked up the cell phone. "I'm walkin' downstairs now."

"Stay on with me," Bryce replied.

"All right." Joe left the bedroom and walked down the hall to the spiral staircase. Joe descended the stairs and stepped to the door. "I'm at the front door."

"Slow and steady, Joe. No sudden movements, okay?"

"Okay."

"Open the door and come out with your hands held up."

"Comin' out." Joe slipped the phone into his pocket and took a deep breath. He opened the door, the spotlight blinding him. He held up his hands and looked down to protect his eyes. Joe made it off the front stoop, only ten feet from the front door, when he was accosted by several officers, pointing their rifles in his direction.

Joe did as he was told, lying on his stomach, and putting his hands on the back of his head. A police officer wrenched his hands behind his back and cuffed them together. Two officers hauled him to his feet and marched him to a waiting cruiser. A short, stocky man in a gray suit stood next to the open door of the cruiser.

"I'm Bryce," the man said.

Joe nodded. "I didn't kill my wife."

"I know you didn't, but you have a lot to answer for."

Joe nodded again. "I can live with that."

Epilogue: Two Years Later ...

Joe was escorted to a visiting room by a CO. The room was filled with perfectly spaced stainless-steel tables with attached stainless-steel disks that functioned as the most uncomfortable seats ever created. Inmates sat at the tables, snacking, talking, laughing, and whispering with their families and friends. A few vending machines lined the walls, with overpriced snacks and sodas. Corrections officers patrolled the room, making sure nobody touched or acted inappropriate or aggressive.

A petite redhead stood from a corner table.

Joe beamed as he approached. He hugged her briefly, not wanting to draw the ire of the COs.

When they separated, Emily smiled back. She resembled Colleen with her high cheekbones, blue eyes, and pale skin. "How are you doing, Dad?"

"Not too bad. I'm more interested in how you're doin'."

She lifted one shoulder. "It's kinda surreal. I don't know how to feel yet."

Joe reached out and squeezed her shoulder. "I'm sorry. I know the trial brought it all up again."

She shook her head. "You don't have anything to be sorry for."

Joe gestured to the table. "Wanna sit?"

They sat across from each other at the square table.

Emily frowned. "I still can't believe she came into our house and did that to Mom. During the trial, I stared at the back of her neck"—Emily lowered her voice—"imagining strangling *her* to death."

Joe whispered back, not wanting the guards to hear. "I get it. I wanted to beat her to death with the butt end of my shotgun." His voice returned to normal. "The only reason I didn't is you."

Emily closed her eyes for a moment. They were glassy when she opened them again. "She almost took you from me too."

Joe reached out and covered her hand with his. "She didn't. I'm here. We're here."

"I thought she was going to get off. If the police hadn't found Mom's DNA on her baton, I think she would've."

Joe nodded and extracted his hand. "You're probably right." Joe thought, *I would've made her pay.*

Emily forced a smile and changed the subject. "You must be getting excited. Only forty-two days left."

Joe smiled back. "I am. I can't wait."

"I'm so happy that you'll be home for Christmas. I already made up the guest room for you."

"I won't stay long. I promise. Just until I start drivin' again."

Emily held up her hand. "Stop. You can stay with us as long as you like. Matty's thrilled. Oh, I almost forgot." She reached into her back pocket and removed a folded piece of paper. She unfolded the paper and slid it across the table.

Joe picked it up and chuckled. "Great picture. Can I keep it?"

"I brought it for you."

The picture showed his four-year-old grandson sleeping on his side, his head on his pillow. A grown-up Baby Kitty slept with him, curled up in his nook.

If you enjoyed this novel, ...
you'll love *Cesspool.*

Would you become a criminal to do the right thing?

Disgraced teacher, James Fisher, moved to a backwoods town, content to live his life in solitude. He was awakened from his apathy by a small girl with a big problem. James suspected Brittany was being abused and exploited by his neighbor. He called the police but soon realized his mistake, as the neighbor was related to the chief of police.

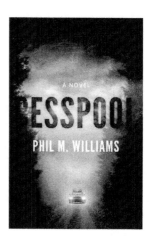

Most would've looked the other way. Getting involved placed James squarely in the crosshairs of the local police. James lacked the brawn or the connections to save himself, much less Brittany. The police held all the power, and they knew it. But that was also their weakness. They underestimated what the mild-mannered teacher and the young runaway would do for justice.

Buy *Cesspool* today if you enjoy vigilante justice page-turners with a side of underdog.
Adult language and content.

What Readers Are Saying

"Wow. Just wow. This book was amazing. Every chapter, every page had me thinking about ideas, philosophies, current events, history in a different way." - Elaine ★★★★★

"The writing is excellent, the pace quick, the characters and dialog believable. An excellent read." - Dusty Sharp, Author of the Austin Conrad Series ★★★★★

"I have enjoyed this author before, but this is his best yet. If you want a story that will keep you reading, this is it. The story, the characters, and the cunning displayed by the hero is some of the best fiction I've had the pleasure to read. Do yourself a favor and pick up this book. You won't lay it down until the end." - Patrick R. ★★★★★

"Wow! This was one of the best books I've read in a while. Twists, turns, and unexpected events in every chapter. What a movie this would make." – Kindle Customer ★★★★★

"This book was incredible! I read it in three days—the entire story is a whirlwind of fantastic characters, a perfect constancy of ups and downs throughout." - Rae L. ★★★★★

For the Reader

Dear Reader,

I'm thrilled that you took precious time out of your life to read my novel. Thank you! I hope you found it entertaining, engaging, and thought-provoking. If so, please consider writing a positive review on Amazon and Goodreads. Five-star reviews have a huge impact on future sales. The review doesn't need to be long and detailed, if you're more of a reader than a writer. As an author and a small businessman, competing against the big publishers, I greatly appreciate every reader, every review, and every referral.

If you're interested in receiving my novel *Against the Grain* for free and/or reading my other titles for free or discounted, go to the following link: http://www.PhilWBooks.com. You're probably thinking, *What's the catch?* There is no catch.

If you want to contact me, don't be bashful. I can be found at Phil@PhilWBooks.com. I do my best to respond to all emails.

Sincerely,
Phil M. Williams

Gratitude

I'd like to thank my wife for being my first reader, sounding board, and cheerleader. Without her support and unwavering belief in my skill as an author, I'm not sure I would have embarked on this career. I love you, Denise.

I'd also like to thank my editors. My developmental editor, Caroline Smailes, did a fantastic job finding the holes in my plot and suggesting remedies. As always, my line editor, Denise Barker (not to be confused with my wife, Denise Williams), did a fantastic job making sure the manuscript was error-free. I love her comments and feedback. Thank you to Deborah Bradseth of Tugboat Design for her excellent cover art and formatting. She's the consummate professional.

Thank you to my beta readers, Sue, Ray, Saundra, and Matteo. They're my last defense against the dreaded typo. Thank you to Patches, Sandy, and Baby Kitty. My real-life feral friends have provided Denise and me with so much more than we've given back in cat food.

And finally, thank you to you, the reader. Without you I wouldn't have a career. As long as you keep reading, I'll keep writing.

Printed in Great Britain
by Amazon

19113982R10089